SPINDLEWOOD BOOKS

The Snow Globe

Anne Merrick was born in Wales. Most of her adult life has been spent in Cheshire and Devon and these areas influence the settings of her writing. She has taught in primary and secondary schools and at Exeter University School of Education. The *Snow Globe* is her third novel for Spindlewood. Her earlier novel *Someone Came Knocking* won a Carnegie commendation.

The Snow Globe

Also by Anne Merrick

SOMEONE CAME KNOCKING
HANNAH'S GHOST

The Snow Globe

Anne Merrick

 Spindlewood

First published in Great Britain in 2001 by
Spindlewood, 70 Lynhurst Avenue,
Barnstaple Devon EX31 2HY

Cover illustration by John Hurford

ISBN 0-907349-24-2

A catalogue record for this book is available from
the British Library.

Typeset by Chris Fayers, Woodford, Cornwall EX23 9JD
Printed and bound in Great Britain by
Short Run Press Ltd., Exeter

For Kirsten, Catherine, Isabel and Anna
who sneak into my stories in various disguises -
with love and gratitude

MONDAY

Chapter 1

Afterwards Bella was to remember how she danced home that afternoon. Light-hearted. In spite of the morning quarrel with Mo. In spite of the dreary day at school without Ali. In spite of the mean, grey February cold. And in spite of the horrible, old-fashioned coat from Oxfam she was wearing.

'But it suits you, Gosling,' Mo had insisted. 'The green shows off your hair and your eyes. And with its high fur collar and full skirt it makes you look like a girl in some wonderful, wintry fairy tale…'

Romantic, ridiculous Mo!

Hop one two three, skip one two three. Bella pranced and twizzled, avoiding the cracks in the pavement. Her breath dragoned out ahead of her, white puffs of steam dissolving quickly into the mistiness of the day. Rounding the corner she entered the cul-de-sac of Pavilion Street. On one side of her was Old Meadow Park and on the other the row of small, terraced houses where she lived. Between bare winter trees the park's grassy slopes were deserted. Even the children's play area was empty. Pushing her frozen hands deep in her pockets Bella leaned against the iron palings and rested there for a moment.

Would Mo still be upset? The quarrel this morning had been a bad one, blowing up out of nowhere as they tended to do nowadays.

'You're hopeless, Mo!' Bella had shouted. 'You're flighty and feckless. You don't take proper *care* of me. You're unfit to be a mother!'

The harsh second-hand words slipped all too easily off her tongue and she saw Mo flinch.

'Quit yelling, Gosling,' she had pleaded. 'You should be past throwing tantrums by now!'

'Past wearing everyone else's cruddy old cast-offs too!' Bella snarled.

But really the coat had only been part of it...

Bella left the railings and arms outstretched as if balancing on a tightrope, she walked carefully along the edge of the grass which marked the park off from the street.

Old Meadow Park. Pavilion Street.

The words, as words often did, triggered a picture in her head. A sunny hillside. A graceful building, flimsy as a tent, glistening white against emerald grass and azure sky. And flying from its pinnacle, a scarlet banner, flapping and snapping in the breeze...

'Hey, you!... Hey, Greensleeves!'

The greeting startled Bella back into the dingy present. She hadn't noticed the boy because he had been standing so still against the trunk of the chestnut tree. And because his clothes were the same drab colour as its bark.

'Hi,' she said. For as soon as he stepped out into the light she recognised him.

'You was in a dream,' said the boy. 'Miles away I should say!'

She smiled at him. *Matty*, she thought. Because although he had told her his name was Matthew, such a straight, sober name did not seem to fit him.

It must have been exactly a week ago. Like today she had been on her way home from school when she saw a group of older boys attack him. They dragged him from the swing where he had tried to escape by climbing on to the crossbar. Then knocking him to the ground they began beating him about his shaven head. Outraged Bella

12

had rushed at once into the fray, getting scratched and kicked herself before Mo, coming to the door of Number 21, saw what was happening and drove the gang away with strong, sharp words and stinging slaps.

Now, looking at him, she thought his head looked horrible shaved to the bone like that. A frail skull out of which his large, green eyes stared boldly at her. There were dark shadows under them and on his right temple, a yellowing bruise.

'Is that from last week?' she asked, reaching out to touch it lightly. 'Or have those bullies beaten you up *again*?'

Bella felt passionately about cruelty of any kind and she hated bullies.

When she was smaller, Sally Vachel, an older girl, used to lie in wait for Bella because she knew Mo never came to meet her from school. At first it was just names. Carrots. Freckles. Snotnose. Sleazebag… Then one day she snatched Bella's schoolbag and flung it over a high wall. She capered around her pinching and punching. Until at last Bella, driven into one of her furies by something Sally said about Mo, had struck her on the chin and almost knocked her out…

Suddenly Matty stroked Bella's coat, taking the cloth between finger and thumb and rubbing it gently.

'What you doing?' she asked, startled.

He drew back but did not answer. Instead he slung his rucksack off his back and delved into it.

'See this,' he said.

And lifting something out of a tissue filled paper bag he placed it in her hands.

Chapter 2

At first Bella thought the object Matty had given her was a paper weight like the one Mo used to anchor the muddle of papers on her desk. Then, as she raised it to catch the light, she saw with a shock of delight that it was something quite different.

It was a glass sphere of just the right size to fit into her cupped hands. Its base was wedged into a rugged block of stone, real rock which still had a caul of dry, golden lichen clinging to it. From this rock, *inside* the glass, a gnarled tree seemed to be growing, its interlacing branches filling the space. As she jiggled it, crystals of snow rose in a flurry, settling on the tree's rough bark and floating down to deepen the drift around its roots. Laughing, Bella shook it up and down, making blizzards whirl and spin, blotting out the tree altogether.

'It's a snow globe,' she cried, remembering the ones she had seen in the shops at Christmas. 'Is it for me?'

The boy's pleased expression abruptly changed. Stepping forward he plucked the globe from her grasp and stooping over his rucksack he buried it once more among its protective tissues.

In the chilly air Bella felt her cheeks flame. Of course the snow globe was not for her! How could she have *imagined* so?

'There you go again,' she could hear Mo saying. 'Heart leap-frogging over head!'

She looked contritely at the boy who had turned away from her and was struggling back into his rucksack. But how had such a scruffy, raggedy boy come by such a beautiful – and surely valuable – thing? The globe was nothing like the cheap plastic toys she had seen in the

14

shops around Christmas time.

'I'm sorry,' she said awkwardly. 'I'll have to go. Mo – my Mum – will be wondering where I am.'

The idea of Mo waiting for her cheered Bella up. That's why she had been dancing home. Because today was Monday and Monday was Mo's day off from the flower shop. The one day she was always home before Bella. 'Like a good old-fashioned Ma, my little Goose! With your supper sizzling on the stove!'

Matty looked crestfallen. And wanting to make up in some way for her silly mistake, she said, 'Come on over and have some tea. Mo won't mind…'

Taking Matty home would be a good way of breaking through any ice left over from the quarrel with her mother. Bella was sure Mo would be pleased to see him again. She had quite taken to him the day they rescued him.

'Such a strange, self-contained little fellow,' she said. 'And not a tear nor a complaint – though those louts really laid into him…'

But glancing across the road to where the bright, buttercup yellow door of Number 21 glowed in the twilight, Matty shook his bald head.

'She ent there,' he said.

Bella stared at him in astonishment. She was about to ask him what he meant when she noticed, for the first time, that there was no light in any of the windows of home.

'Oh, no!' she exclaimed, stamping her foot. 'Surely she's not forgotten it's Monday!'

She thought she heard Matty snicker with suppressed laughter and she stormed away from him, all the dance gone out of her. As she crossed the street he called something after her but without looking back she headed swiftly for the end house. Through the front window she saw the living room was dark and empty, no flicker of flames in the grate, no light from the kitchen showing through the open door.

'Hell!' she swore, breaking all Mo's strict rules about swearing. 'Bloody, bloody hell!'

Then taking the key from where it was strung on a chain around her neck she stabbed it into the lock as if she wanted to kill it.

Chapter 3

Ten minutes later, with her temper steamed off, Bella sprawled on the sagging couch in the living room and picked moodily at the threads of the Indian bedspread which covered it.

'If only you were a *proper* grown-up, Mo!' she said to her absent mother.

Except really she loved Mo the way she was. In the good times it was fun having a mother who was more like an older sister. Who did wild, madcap, unexpected things and then sat and giggled with you about them afterwards.

It was only in the bad times that it troubled Bella. The times when there was no money to pay the bills; when the bailiffs came and took the television *again*; when the visiting social workers whispered darkly about Bella going into care; when Mo played truant from work and Mrs Jenkins, who owned the flower shop, threatened to sack her (but Mo was so brilliant at her job that she never had – yet); or when, as now, Mo simply wasn't around…

'I'd so looked forward to a special, *forgiving* supper

tonight,' mourned Bella.

She wondered if Mo were staying away to punish her for the quarrel but it was not in either of their natures to sulk or bear grudges for long.

Thinking of supper reminded Bella she was cold and hungry. Whistling to cheer herself up she went into the kitchen and unlocked the back door. Out in the small back yard she could see the first star, hanging above the spire of St Barnabas' Church. The stars at least were steady and dependable! In just the same place her mother must have seen this one when *she* was a child. Mo had lived in this house ever since she was born. She gave birth to Bella here. She saw her own mother die here. And from here she said goodbye to her father when he emigrated to Canada to live with her brother, Simon.

At least, thought Bella, that means no-one can take the house from us. For her grandfather had given it to Mo when he left.

Crossing to the outhouse she fetched kindling (collected by her and Mo on their country walks) and a bucket of coal. Back in the living room the dry sticks flared quickly into life. Shadows jigged among the tatty furniture which Mo had painted in creams and golds, strong yellows and burnt orange. And above Bella's head bunches of dried flowers, dangling from the ceiling, swayed in the updraught, their brittle stalks squeaking together like the conversation of mice.

She began to clear the table under the window. It was cluttered with Mo's sewing machine and heaped with bright scraps of material. Just like Mo to leave it all lying around! She was making a patchwork quilt for Bella's birthday in March and it was supposed to be a secret.

'But it was a *bike* I wanted,' Bella had wailed that

morning. 'One like Ali's with loads of gears and lilac mudguards!'

'I can't, Gosling. There simply isn't enough money in the kitty!'

'Why isn't there? You told me you were saving up. Where's it all *gone*…?'

Mo shook her head helplessly. Bella knew she did not earn a great deal making wedding bouquets and funeral wreaths and concocting fantastical flower arrangements for Fat Cats' Feasts (Mo's words) but the truth was Mo was hopeless with money. It vanished from purse and pocket as though some airy, invisible Magician were constantly conjuring it away. In its place appeared shining samples of silk and velvet (for making patchwork); tins of marigold paint (for 'livening up' the house); glitzy earrings and gauzy scarves; art books, poetry books – and sometimes expensive treats like pheasant or smoked salmon for supper.

'If only I had a Dad!' Bella had raged. '*He'd* buy me a bike. *And* I could go on the school trip to France next term!'

Ali could coax anything out of *her* father. Not that Bella wanted a father like Mr Whiddon. He was much too gruff and hairy and he talked of nothing except football…

At the mention of a Dad, Mo had started to hum – the way she did when she was angry or upset. You couldn't argue with a hum so Bella had grabbed her schoolbag and flounced out of the house, banging the door behind her.

Now, as she folded away the last piece of sky blue silk, Bella heard footsteps outside and then the door knocker banged three times against the door. Her heart lifted. Mo, she thought. At last!

'Trust you to have forgotten your key,' she muttered as she drew the door open.

But it wasn't Mo. It was Mrs Parker from next door. *Nosy* Parker.

'Would your Ma let me have a cup of sugar d'you think, lover? Just till I can get to the shop?'

'I'll ask her,' said Bella.

The old witch! She knows Mo's not here!

Trekking back into the kitchen Bella half closed the door.

'It's Mrs Parker,' she announced loudly to the Mo who wasn't there. 'Come to borrow some sugar.'

Then she hummed like Mo and seconds later returned with a cracked cup.

'Sorry,' she said. 'Mo says we've only got demerara.'

She knew Mrs Parker didn't like brown sugar. The woman peered past her down the unlit hall.

'Having your tea then?'

'Yes,' lied Bella. 'We're in the middle of it.'

She began to shut the door but Mrs Parker didn't budge. She had a floss of faded blonde hair and enormous bulges everywhere.

('Her boobs and her bum!' giggled Mo's voice in Bella's head. 'They balance perfectly!')

'I'll bring your cup back later then.'

'No need,' said Bella, edging the door onwards, nudging it against Mrs Parker's foot. 'Any time will do...'

When she had gone Bella fetched herself bread to toast by the fire. Switching on the television she pinned a slice of bread to the prongs of Mo's long kitchen fork and knelt on the hearthrug, oohing and ouching as her fingers grew too hot.

From the television screen the commercials chattered

19

and blared.

'Come on, come on,' she muttered. 'Let's have the Golden Sunbursts ad. Let me see my Dad!'

But the last word sounded false and awkward in her mouth and turning the burning bread she said quickly, 'I mean – let's see *Oliver*!'

In this set of advertisements, however, there was no slot for Golden Sunbursts. So Oliver did not appear. And Bella, buttering the toast and spreading Marmite thickly, let the programme roll while she turned to the inside of her head where Oliver had lately taken up residence.

Chapter 4

Bella's father disappeared out of her life six months before she was born, when Mo was just seventeen. Bella had hardly given him a thought until after her grandfather emigrated. Then, missing *him* badly, she found herself wondering about her father.

'What was he like?' she asked Mo. 'Tell me about him.'

But Mo clearly did not want to say.

'He was a RAT, Gosling,' she said. 'Not worth two ticks of our time talking about him!'

'If he was a rat,' mused Bella, 'I must be half a rat.'

Mo's smoky-blue eyes narrowed and she ran her fingers through her bobbed auburn hair. 'Well,' she murmured, 'I suppose he wasn't *all* rat. Or I wouldn't have fallen in love with him.'

'Was he good looking?'

Mo shrugged.

'What was his name? At least tell me his name?'

'Just his name. Then no more questions, right?'

'Right.'

'His name was Oliver,' said Mo. And giggled.

After that she would say no more. She wouldn't even say whether Oliver was his first name or his surname.

Bella Oliver, thought Bella. How gross! It sounded like the beginning of some slithery tongue twister. Better to be Bella Partridge. The worst that Ali and the crowd at school could do with that was to call her Birdie!

The only other thing which Mo ever let slip was that when he deserted her, Bella's father had gone to London. To drama school.

Then, one evening about a fortnight ago, when she and Bella were having supper together and waiting for the commercials to finish so that a nature film about urban foxes could continue, Mo had suddenly shot upright and shrieked, 'Oliver! Blow me if that isn't Oliver Montford!'

Bella had choked on a grain of rice and by the time she had stopped coughing the commercial was over and Mo was in one of her 'touch and talk to me not' sort of moods. But since then, whenever Mo was out, Bella had watched the commercials avidly. She had seen the one for Golden Sunbursts five times and knew it by heart. There was only one man in it. Oliver. And he did not *look* like a rat. He was smallish and slender with close cropped curly hair that was beginning to grey over his temples. His face was sharp and intelligent-looking and (like Bella herself) he had a crooked smile.

In the film he was looking after his young son. He was preparing a special meal – to show what a *good* father he was. As he whipped eggs and chopped mushrooms you could see, through the billowing net curtains behind him, a field of ripened wheat, dazzling gold in the sun.

21

The action then cut to the evening. The kitchen table was laid with blue and white china. When the boy burst in through the door Oliver served up his supper with a flourish. But the boy refused to eat. Oliver coaxed and cajoled. There was a close up of his face, half-rueful, half-amused, his tawny eyes glinting with hidden laughter.

Huh, thought Bella. At this point she always lost interest because after carrying the boy up to bed, Oliver left and did not re-appear.

Scrambling up on to the settee, she stretched out and closed her eyes to dream. On the screen the boy whistled a little tune and at once a Genie came whooshing through curtains bearing a bowl of Golden Sunbursts. The cereal crackled and fizzed with light. A seraphic expression came over the boy's face and he gobbled it all up…

Chapter 5

It was a long time later when Bella woke up. The fire had died down to a dull smoulder and the late news was ending on the television. Rubbing her eyes she sat up and looked at the clock on the mantelpiece. Ten-twenty it said.

WHERE ON EARTH WAS MO?

Although Mo often went out in the evening – sometimes to chat with friends over coffee, sometimes to go to an evening class or the cinema, she never went out at night without telling Bella where she was going.

Feeling lonely and vaguely uneasy, Bella took her supper things into the kitchen and slid them into the sink. Beside her the telephone perched on the wall like a dead green parrot. She picked it up but there was not the faintest buzz of life. They had been cut off for weeks.

Wondering if she had overlooked a note from Mo, she spent five minutes searching in the usual places. There was no note. She yawned and poking the fire to a feeble blaze she sat on the rug again and tried to read a Point Horror book Ali had lent her. But every noise from outside made her tense, waiting for the sound of Mo's key in the lock. It did not come. In the end she decided the only thing to do was to go out and 'phone Mo's friends.

Number 21 was the last house in the terrace. Beyond it there was only a narrow alley way which climbed steeply between high brick walls to Upper Park Road. The telephone box lay in the other direction, outside St Barnabas' Church Hall. Bella scurried along keeping close to the houses. She wished she'd been reading something funny, not something frightening.

Where the green slopes of the park rose to meet the walls of the old City Hospital there was an ancient cemetery. Neglected and overgrown it made a patch of deeper darkness under the trees that had grown like giant weeds among the tombstones. A little breeze shivered their branches and they creaked eerily. It seemed a long way to the telephone.

Sometimes, by arrangement, Mo would ring Bella here. But today there had been no such arrangement. As she entered the booth Bella wondered what to say. She did not want Mo's friends to know she was missing. Bella took care never to give *anyone* the chance to be sniffy about her mother. Setting out a row of ten pence pieces she decided to pretend to be ringing from Ali's house.

'Ali's Mum says I can sleep over here,' she said to Juno

who sounded half asleep. 'I need to let Ma know but I've forgotten where she said she'd be this evening…'

'Not here, Bell,' yawned Juno. 'She's not here. Haven't you left it rather late? D'you want me to pop down and see if she's back? Slip a note through the door for her if she isn't?'

'No. No need,' said Bella hastily. 'I've just remembered. I think she's at Sal's…'

The lies flowed smoothly. She was used to telling them. At school and out of it she was always covering up for Mo. Partly out of loyalty and partly because, as Mo said, 'We don't want Social Services to come snooping, Gosling. If they suspect I'm neglecting you they'll cart you off into care faster than I can run to your rescue!'

Mo was not with any of her friends. As Bella finished speaking to the last one, a young woman, arms and legs bare to the cold night air, pressed her nose against the glass door of the booth and mouthed 'Hurry up!'

Bella left. The grass was sheened with frost and in the sky the stars were sharp as needle points. A hundred metres ahead, under the streetlamp outside Number 21, the shadows shifted and she thought she saw someone standing, waiting.

'Mo?' she cried. And started to run.

A small figure, too small for Mo, slipped out of the circle of light and turned the corner into the alley way. Bella was about to follow when the door of Number 19 opened.

'Who's there?' called Mrs Parker, peering into the dark. 'Was that you I heard, lover?'

Bella stopped and Mrs Parker stepped into the street, all her bulges bobbing indignantly.

'What you blessed well doing out here alone?' she

demanded.

'I went to 'phone my friend Ali.'

'What! At this time of night?' huffed Mrs Parker. 'Your Mam must be mad to allow it!'

Bridling at the criticism, Bella said, 'Mo doesn't know. She went to bed early with a bad cold.'

Mrs Parker's lips set in a prim line among her folds of flesh.

'If the truth were known,' she said, 'I believe you're becoming as much of a little madam as she is! And if she's not careful you'll come to the same sort of bad end! You mark my words…'

'Mo hasn't come to any sort of an end,' fumed Bella. 'It's just a bad *cold* she's got!'

And without waiting to hear more she pushed open the door of Number 21, shutting it firmly behind her. But later, as she prepared for bed in the silent, empty house, Mrs Parker's words came back to her and struck chill to her heart.

'Where *are* you, Mo?' she pleaded. 'Please come home soon!'

TUESDAY

Chapter 6

Bella slept badly. Each time she jolted awake out of tangled dreams she padded along the landing to Mo's room to see if she was back. Then, as it grew light, she fell into a deep sleep and did not wake until half-past eight.

With her head feeling as if it were stuffed with cotton wool, she choked down a bowl of cornflakes. No Golden Sunbursts for her. No Oliver, either, to make her delicious sandwiches. Instead she grabbed two Ryvita biscuits and the last of the cheese and together with a bruised apple she threw them into her lunch box.

School smelled of stale dinners, sweat and chalk dust. Bella scrambled into her place just as Miss Fairfax began the register. About a third of the class, including Ali, were missing.

'Which of you have already had chicken pox?' asked Miss Fairfax.

Several hands shot up. Bella said she didn't know. Miss Fairfax pursed her lips. As clearly as if she had spoken her expression said, 'Well! With Mo Partridge for a mother I'm not surprised. She probably wouldn't notice if you'd got spots the size of pound coins!'

Tall and willowy with glossy black hair tied neatly on the nape of her neck, Helen Fairfax looked much older than Mo. But as children they had been in the same class at St Barnabas' school.

'Not that we were ever exactly friends, Gosling,' said Mo. 'She was clean and clever and conscientious – while I was the scruffy class clown!'

There's no way, thought Bella, *I can tell Miss Fairfax about Mo*.

The day was dull, dreary drab, dismal…

The words multiplied easily in Bella's head as she struggled to multiply fractions. Then, between Maths and History, she suddenly *knew* that when she arrived home Mo would be there waiting for her. Breathless, apologetic, her blue eyes simmering with a mixture of laughter and remorse. They would hug each other and Bella would breathe in flowery perfume and Mo's own warm smell of milk and honey.

Later, however, as she drew a picture of Henry VIII (who looked like a beer barrel with a crested bird perched on top of it) she was swept again with doubt and fear. What if something dreadful had happened to Mo? What if she'd been taken hostage by a gang of desperate criminals? Or what if…?

'Bella,' said Miss Fairfax, pausing beside her. 'Leaving aside the blotchiness of your work, Henry had six wives, not eight. And they weren't *all* beheaded. That would have been over the top, even for him!'

Her voice was warm, her tone amused and for one dizzy moment Bella thought of confessing her problem. Then everything steadied. If Mo were a normal mother, or if it were anyone other than Mo who'd gone missing, she knew she'd have to tell *someone*. But being Mo, it was perhaps better to wait a little longer. At least until tomorrow…

Chapter 7

Not wanting to go home, not wanting to know for certain yet whether Mo was back or not, Bella dawdled along Pavilion Street. Clouds hung in dust-coloured drapes low over the rooftops and trails of smoke rose raggedly from the chimneys to mingle with them.

Depressing, she thought.

There were a few toddlers in the play area today chasing each other round the climbing frame, making wide figures of eight while their mothers chatted beside the fence. Under the chestnut tree, instead of Matty, an old man stood with his dog. Bella knew him. He lived at the far end of the street, next to the church hall. She stopped and stroked his dog.

'Arternoon, Maidy,' he said. 'I were just contemplating this yere park.'

'Mm?'

'Aye,' he went on. ''Twere once a fresh green valley with a stream o' sparkling water running through it.' He pointed up the hill to the hospital and the graveyard. 'There were a leper house thereabouts,' he said. 'And they used to bury 'n up yonder because in they days it were well outside Orbury city walls. That were long afore my time o' course!'

He gave a throaty chuckle and Bella smiled. She already knew all this because he had told her several times before.

'You shouldn't loiter out yere, Maidy,' he said moving on and tugging the dog after him. 'Not now 'tis growing dimpsy. There's some peculiar characters as hang about this park…'

Yes, thought Bella, remembering the figure under the lamp-post last night. Frowning, she stood and watched the children playing for a while before she crossed the road. Poking like a white tongue from the letter box of Number 21 was a slip of paper. Bella's heart lifted. Perhaps it was a note from Mo. Perhaps she'd rushed down from the shop in her dinner hour and left it there for Bella.

31

Opening the door she drew it through. But instead of a message from Mo, it was a message *for* her.

Dear Morag, it said.

This is the <u>second</u> time I've called today. Where might I ask, <u>are</u> you? Have you forgotten there are urgent orders to be dealt with – most importantly the Tremlett funeral on Thursday and the flower arrangements for the Feniton dinner on Friday evening. Unless I hear from you before closing time <u>tonight</u> you can consider yourself without a job. You rely too much on my goodness of heart, Morag. There are plenty more fish in the sea, you know!

Yours,

Meg Jenkins.

'Might as well rely on a viper's goodness of heart,' muttered Bella, noting how Mrs Jenkins' underlinings had scored right through the thin paper. Crumpling the note in one hand she closed the door with the other and bawled Mo's name. There was no response.

'Bugs and bogles!' she swore.

Since Mo would not allow swearing, Bella, who needed words to shape her anger, had invented her own.

'Flowers with Flair' was half way up Southgate Hill. In the window bronze and gold and pink chrysanthemums clustered together among dark foliage. Outside on the pavement the first fragile flowers of spring, daffodils and narcissi, were bunched in plastic buckets.

Bella took a deep breath and went in. Mrs Jenkins was serving a customer and Flo, the Work Experience girl, was sweeping the shop floor. Guessing why Bella had come, she grinned. Bella shuffled from one foot to the other while excuses for Mo chased each other through her head.

Funeral (but whose?). Fever (but what kind?). Food poisoning (chicken pie or prawns?). Fainting fits. Frothing at the mouth. Rabies. Mad cow disease…

'So what is it this time, Bella Donna?'

Mrs Jenkins bustled towards her, unsmiling. She always gave this extra name to Bella. Mo said it meant 'beautiful gift' but Miss Fairfax had told them it was the Latin name for deadly nightshade. As Mrs Jenkins dealt in plants and did not like children, Bella thought it more likely she meant *that*.

'I'm sorry Mrs Jenkins,' she began. 'I was supposed to come and tell you this morning but I was late for school… because Mo's ill…'

A look of disbelief arched Mrs Jenkins' painted eyebrows and deepened the powdery creases round her mouth.

'With chicken pox,' said Bella, suddenly inspired. 'Everyone's got it, you know. It's like the plague! I expect Mo caught it from my best friend, Ali.' Her glance slid to Flo who was smirking behind a vase of white lilies. 'And now she's covered in bright red spots,' she finished. 'Like Flo's apron!'

'Right,' said Mrs Jenkins, grimly. 'I'll come and see her after work.'

Bella's throat tightened. 'No,' she squeaked. 'I shouldn't do that. She's horribly infectious and her throat's so swollen she can hardly speak.'

Mrs Jenkins' pale blue eyes were cold.

'I hope you've called the doctor,' she said.

'Yes,' mumbled Bella, feeling herself becoming more and more entangled in the web of lies she was weaving. 'But he's so busy – with the epidemic – he hasn't been able to see her yet…'

The shop doorbell rang and another customer came in. As she turned to serve him Mrs Jenkins said, 'Tell your mother I shall expect a sick note before the end of the week. Otherwise she needn't bother coming back. Understand?'

Bella nodded. Then scowling ferociously at the Work Experience girl she backed out of the shop.

Oh Mo, she thought. *I hate all this! Why do you get me into such snarlygogging messes!*

Chapter 8

It was already dark by the time Bella went to the outhouse to fetch wood for the fire. Tonight the clouds had hidden the evening star and all she could see was the floodlit spire of St Barnabas' Church pointing like a warning finger at the sky.

'I wish I believed in you, God,' she murmured. 'Then, at least, I could ask *you* for help!' But it was not so much that she didn't believe in God as that she could not *imagine* Him.

Setting down her bucket she reached for the latch on the door. As soon as she touched it, from inside the shed, she heard a rustle and then a louder scrabbling sound.

Rats!

There were rats, people said, all over this quarter of the city. Huge, sleek creatures that lived in the tunnels and underground caverns which had once been part of Orbury's drainage system. And last winter Mo herself had seen one in the yard.

'Scram!' yelled Bella, rattling the latch to scare the rat away. Then wrenching the door open she stood well back.

Instead of a small, furry animal scuttling among the coals, however, a small, blurry boy came staggering out into the yard. Masked by dusk and coal dust, he was wearing a black baseball cap which covered his baldness. But she knew at once who it was.

'What's *with* you!' she cried. '*Stalking* me like this! How come you're in our shed now?'

With jerky, puppet movements Matty straightened his stiff limbs.

'I come over the wall,' he said. 'It's easy from the alley…'

'But why?'

''Cos they wus after me agin.'

'Who was after you?'

'George and Arnie and them. The Gang.'

'The same boys Mo drove away the other day?'

'Uh-huh.'

Matty sat down on the doorstep, took off his cap and beat it against the wall until the dust flew. Bella squatted in front of him.

'So what've you done?' she demanded. 'To make them persecute you like this?'

'They's allus after me,' he shrugged. 'It's just the way they are!'

She peered into his coal-blackened face. In the light from the kitchen she saw he had a fresh cut on his cheek bone. Against his pale skin it looked raw and angry.

'Were you in the park last night?' she asked. 'Was it you – standing there under the lamp – when I went out?'

Matty did not answer but stared steadily back at her, his eyes glittering greenish gold, like a cat's. Then his lips stretched wide over small, pointed white teeth.

Bella drew back. She thought he hardly looked like a

human child at all. He reminded her of a story Mo once told her. It was about a baby whose mother had carelessly fallen asleep as she watched beside his cradle. And while she slept goblins had crept into the house and stolen him away. In his place they left one of their own. At first the mother saw no difference but as the boy grew he turned more and more awry and strange. A goblin child. A changeling...

'Where d'you come from?' she asked Matty uneasily. 'What you doing here? Why don't you go home and tell your Mum about the... the bullying?'

Matty gave a thin, high cackle of laughter and stood up, pushing wide the kitchen door.

'When you give us some tea,' he said. 'I'll tell you.'

When, noted Bella, *not if*. She admired his cheek anyway.

In the end it was Matty who cooked the supper while Bella lit the fire. He stirred a can of baked beans and sausages into another of spaghetti. Then, because the only bread left in the house was half a currant loaf, he toasted thick wedges of that to go with it. Finally he peeled and quartered the last orange, scattered chocolate chips over it and topped it up with a large dollop of strawberry yoghurt.

The tea he made was the colour of dark toffee and into his own he stirred three teaspoons of icing sugar.

'That were yummy,' he said, smacking his lips and pushing away the plates.

They were sitting side by side on the hearthrug, their backs against the settee, their toes stretched towards the fire.

'This room's kinda... kinda like a summer garden,' he

said. 'I likes it.' He took a last gulp of tea and twisted his fingers into the stuff of the rug which Mo had made by weaving scraps of material into a piece of sacking.

'What's this flower?' he asked.

'Sunflower. Mo thinks Van Gogh's the greatest!'

'Van Goff? Is he a pop star?'

'No,' giggled Bella. 'But never mind about him. You said you'd tell me about yourself.' She was impatient for Matty to talk and so drive out the miserable voice in her head which kept nagging, 'Where is Mo? What are you going to do about Mo?'

Already she had discovered he was not much of a talker. That he only spoke when he had something necessary to say. Considering this it was odd how comfortable she felt with him. Nevertheless he disconcerted her when, instead of answering her, he curled up in a ball hiding his face against his knees.

'Ent nothin' to tell,' he mumbled.

This was not true. There was plenty to tell but Matty did not want to dwell on it. He spent much of his life distracting himself from it and saw no point in upsetting Bella or himself by going into details.

Irked by his continuing silence Bella nudged him sharply.

'Come on,' she said. 'I've kept my side of the bargain. You've had a great tea!'

'Luscious,' he agreed. And burped loudly.

'At least tell me where you live.'

He squirmed. 'If you must know,' he muttered, 'I lives at Elmbridge House.'

'What? Elmbridge House – the children's home?'

'Yep.'

'Haven't you got any Mum or Dad then? Are you an

37

orphan?' Bella was appalled. To have only one parent was bad enough. To have none must be so lonely. *So unprotected*!

Matty shook his head. His mother was dead but he had a father somewhere. As he tried to explain this to Bella a lost, long ago memory came stealing into his mind.

He was walking along a hot, dusty road, his small hand engulfed in a much larger one. He felt tired and thirsty but somehow safe and happy at the same time. Then he stumbled over a stone and his father, grasping him by the arms, swung him high on to his shoulders. Riding there Matty could hear a deep voice rumbling away beneath him but could not hear the words for laughing. This was because, as his father's jaws moved up and down, his golden beard tickled Matty's bare legs…

'But in any case,' Bella was protesting, 'Elmbridge House is miles away. On the other side of Orbury. What are you doing coming here – to Old Meadow Park all the time?'

'I doesn't.'

'You do. You're here now. And this is the third time I've seen you here!'

Uncoiling himself, Matty plucked at the yellow petals of Mo's sunflower. 'That first time,' he said, 'I just come to the Park. But ever afterwards I come to see *you*.'

'ME?' Bella started at him, dumbfounded, and saw his sallow face slowly flush brick-red.

'I comes to see you,' he repeated, without looking at her, ''Cos I reckons you're my… you're my Destiny…'

Chapter 9

DESTINY

To Bella the word seemed to hang before them printed in fiery letters. It was such an unlikely word for Matty to use. Did he, she wondered, even know what it meant?

To Matty himself it was a magical word. He liked the sound of it, the feel of it in his mouth. Its meaning was slightly misty and mysterious and he liked that too. But it was also quite simple. Because ever since he could remember he had known that one day he would find a special person of his own. The right person. His destiny.

All he had been waiting for was a sign. And ten days ago, when Bella had rushed into his fight with the Gang, hair like a burning bush, coat as green as holly, he had been given that sign. Plain as the nose on his face.

He knew it was too soon to try to explain this to her. All he could do was to offer her a clue and see what she made of it.

Dragging his rucksack from where he'd left it on the couch, he rummaged inside it. Beside him Bella fidgeted impatiently. Longing to hear more she guessed he was not going to tell her. When he drew the snow globe once again from its brown paper bag she felt disappointed.

'You has to look at it *properly*,' he said, sensing this.

Puzzled, Bella took it between her hands and stared into it as if it were a crystal ball. In the bright light of the living room she saw the glass had a greenish cast. And the tree inside it appeared to shimmer and waver as though she were looking at it through deep, clear water. Its leafless branches twisted upwards and outwards in a dense net through which the light filtered like clouded sunshine.

'Turn it,' said Matty, watching her face. Slowly Bella did. Then she gasped with surprise. For standing beneath the tree on the other side was a human figure. She only had time to take in that the figure was dressed in green, before Matty, leaning across her, ran his finger over the globe and showed her where there was a moon shaped flaw in the glass.

'Put this one right agin your eye,' he said.

Obeying him she took a moment to focus. The shaken snow separated itself into flakes, each one magnified to show its unique, crystaline shape. Behind their slow downward drift, the tree blurred but the human figure seemed to spring forward.

'A girl!' cried Bella. 'Like me!'

For the girl's hair flamed against the grey of the tree bark and her long holly green coat swirled around her ankles where the snow lapped over her boots. One arm hung at her side, the hand hidden in a fur muff which matched her turned up collar. The other reached up towards the tree where a robin, its fluffed out breast as red as her hair, perched on a lower branch and regarded her with a beady eye.

'So that's it,' murmured Bella, not sure quite what she meant. Her eye ached against the cold glass and she lowered the globe on to her lap. Snow whirled, speckling the girl's hair, the grooved and crumpled tree bark.

Content to let her think about it, Matty took it from her.

'Where did you get it from?' she asked.

Matty raised the globe to his own eye. Peeped through a different flaw in the glass. Saw something she had not seen and smiled to himself.

'Me Gran give it to me,' he said.

40

Bella shook her head and thinking she did not believe him, he said, 'She did so! She give it me when… when they took me away…'

'Took you away?'

'To the Home. Me Gran couldn't cope, see.'

'But what happened to your Mum… your Dad?'

Matty began to pack the snow globe back into its bag.

'Me Dad pushed off. He were a bricklayer and he couldn't find no work here. So he went to Germany. But he never come back and after that me Mam was allus ill. Well, she drank a lot, see. And in the end she dumped me on me Gran…'

The fire hissed and a gassy blue flame jetted from a crag of coal. Matty stared into it and thought about his Gran. Her hazy blue eyes whose gaze seemed always fixed on the past, her mouth crimped up with the pain in her back. She could hardly walk, let alone run, those times when he took off…

'I've *never* had a Dad,' said Bella, wanting to show sympathy but boasting a little too.

'You ent got a Mam now, neither,' he said.

Bella's heart gave a painful lurch and the fear she had been keeping at bay all day gripped it like ice. She leapt to her feet.

'Where on earth can Mo have got to?' she cried, clenching her fists. 'She's never left me like this before!'

'Mebbe she's gone off,' he suggested. 'With her man…'

'Her MAN!' Bella was outraged. 'Mo hasn't got a man!'

Restlessly she paced the room, dragging her fingers across the furniture as she passed. Once, long ago, there had been someone. His name was Steve. He had a bristly beard and an infectious, chuckling laugh. He called at the house to take Mo out and sometimes he came to supper.

41

Then suddenly he appeared at breakfast one morning and after that he stayed. He played football with Bella and Mo in the park.

'Come on my Beauties,' he teased them. 'Let's see if you can beat the Beast today!'

When he pushed her on the swing he made it fly so high that the chains kinked and rattled, the seat leapt, and she was deliciously scared. Occasionally he took her and Mo in his old Mini and they went for a picnic on the moors or by the sea.

Often though he was absent for days at a time and when he came back he was gruff and bad-tempered, swearing and slurring his words. Then one night he hit Mo and soon after that he disappeared altogether. Through tears, Mo said, 'I told him to choose between me and the beer, Gosling. And the beer won. I swear he's the last, the very last, man ever to cross this threshold.'

And so he had been.

Bella's silence filled the room. Matty, who was not at all perturbed by it but whose own thoughts had been following a very different track, suddenly said, 'You better be careful, Greensleeves. If your Mam don't turn up soon and *They* gets to know, They'll take you away an' all. Into Care... like me.'

Under the lamp his bony head shone white and his eyes were hollowed out with shadow. To Bella he looked like some bloodless creature risen from the dark underworld of her fears.

'Go away,' she said, pausing in her walk. 'I don't know why I ever let you in. Get out of my life and quit bugging me. Clear off to wherever you came from!'

Well used to such abuse – and worse – Matty scarcely blinked. He was not even disappointed in Bella,

42

recognising that her sudden nastiness came out of her own pain. It was a pattern he saw repeated over and over again, might have been guilty of himself, if it were not for his Gran.

'Don't ee ever let me ketch you doin' that, Matt,' she would say, shaking her stick at him. 'I reckon there's enough nat'ral misery in this old world without us passin' on what's dealt to us – like some sort o' cursed parcel…'

Smiling to himself at the memory he hitched his rucksack on to his shoulder, pulled his baseball cap low over his eyes and without another word, left.

WEDNESDAY

Throughout the whole of the long day at school Bella kept lapsing into daydreams about Mo.

Mo dancing home, triumphant, wheeling a lilac-coloured bicycle.

Mo brought home, despondent, by the police.

Mo strolling beside a turquoise tropical sea, stooping now and then to pick up a delicate, coiled shell for her collection.

Mo trapped in some dark, evil-smelling place, feeling hungry, frightened, lonely, lost…

When the dreams slid like that towards nightmare she switched to safer, more familiar, fantasies about Oliver.

PE was the last lesson on a Wednesday and when Miss Fairfax made them lie down and relax bone by bone until they sprawled, limp as jellyfish, on the hard gym floor, Bella, worn out, almost drifted off to sleep.

I can't face going home, she thought. *I'm going to visit Ali.*

Ali's house on Torsham Road was opposite County Hall, headquarters of the Social Workers. Tossing her head in their direction Bella swung in through the gate. With luck Mrs Whiddon would ask her to stay to tea. Ali's mother never said anything about Mo but her special kindness to Bella implied somehow, that she felt Mo was less than satisfactory as a mother. Bella did not intend to tell her of Mo's absence but at the same time she half hoped that Ali's family might winkle the information out of her.

She had almost reached the front door when Ali's little sister, Lou, poked her head out of an upstairs window.

'Birdie!' she shrieked. 'Go home! Everyone's *catching* in here! We've all got chicken spots!'

'Isn't Ali better yet?' asked Bella.

'No,' said Lou, solemnly. 'Actually, she's getting worser and worser!'

'Where's your Mum?'

'Out. Shopping.'

'Come on down, Lou. Let me in. I don't care about the chicken pox.'

'No way!' exclaimed Lou, looking shocked. 'Not allowed.'

The curtain was pulled aside and Bella saw Ali's head appear beside her sister's. Signalling with her hands Bella pleaded to be let in.

'I need to talk to you,' she said. And in desperation added, 'Secrets!'

Ali loved secrets. But pointing to her face which was covered in crusty spots and painted white like a clown's with calamine, Ali croaked, 'I can't. I'm itching all over. Even inside my mouth. And talking hurts!'

Then, before Bella could argue, she drew the window shut and vanished.

'Abandoned,' murmured Bella as she set off back down the hill. 'Deserted. Forsaken. Dumped…'

But strangely, the pictures the words conjured up were pictures of Matty, not of herself.

Above her head the wind wailed in the telegraph wires. It sounded to Bella like the forlorn crying of some lost spirit. Turning up her collar, she nestled her chin into its warm fur. Number 21 would be bleak and cheerless tonight. Unless, of course, Mo had returned.

The hope quickened her footsteps and she was almost running by the time she reached the shop at the corner of Chapel Street.

'Going to be a wild night by the sound of it!' said Mrs Digby as, taking the last of Bella's pocket money, she packed bread and eggs and cheese into a carrier bag.

Pausing outside St Barnabas' church hall, Bella watched the tops of the trees in the park toss and sway against the massing clouds. A boy came out of the telephone booth, glanced at her and then hurried away. She was just moving on when the telephone started to ring. She looked back but there was nobody waiting for a call. Nobody else about at all. What if that were Mo, trying to contact her?

In a fluster of blown coat and dropped schoolbag, Bella tugged at the glass door. Grabbing the receiver off its hook she listened. But no one spoke.

'Who… who's there?' she said.

There was a stifled exclamation at the other end and then someone with a rough, gritty voice said, 'Is that you, Birdie?'

A tingling feeling like an electric shock ran from Bella's heart to her finger tips. 'Yes,' she whispered.

'Right. Well listen, Birdie. We knows exactly what's going on. We knows *everything*…' Stricken with fright Bella was lost for words but the voice snarled on, 'Don't mess wiv us, Birdie. You give us you-know-what by this time tomorrer, or else…'

Bella tried to interrupt, to ask who they were and what it was they wanted, but her voice was frozen in her throat and in any case the person at the other end was not listening.

''Till this time tomorrer, Birdie,' he repeated. 'Or ELSE!'

There followed a string of ugly oaths and then the line went dead.

Chapter 11

An hour later Bella sat in her coat by the ashes of yesterday's fire. She was still shaking and the raw telephone voice kept repeating its meaningless but threatening message in her head.

'Tomorrow, Birdie. Or else.'

Had someone kidnapped Mo? But why? It couldn't be for her money! And what was Bella supposed to do? Should she have received some earlier message which would explain it?

Groaning she curled up tight. She had never been so miserable.

'I should have gone to the police,' she moaned.

Sometimes she felt more like Mo's mother than her daughter. But in this case she had not behaved like a mother. She knew that if she, Bella, had been missing for three days, Mo would long ago have told the police.

'If I'd gone to the police, though,' she said to herself, 'they'd say "Oh ho! What have we here? Mo Partridge neglecting her child again. Going off without a word and leaving her home alone. Tut. Tut. Tut." And they'd shovel me straight into Care…'

The wind whiffled through the gaps between the window and its frame and its shrill, gossiping voice seemed to mock her.

'I need you Mo!' she cried aloud. 'I need you to tell me what to do!'

After that she did not know how long she went on sitting there before she heard someone knock on the door. Jumping up she stumbled on pins and needly legs and went to answer it. Buffeted by the gale the door crashed open almost knocking her over. Under the thrashing trees the streetlamp flickered like a candleflame and it took her a moment to see who was there.

'Are you all right, lover?' asked Mrs Parker hugging herself against the cold. Was there concern as well as curiosity in her sharp brown eyes? Weakened by tears and tiredness, Bella wavered.

'No,' murmured Mo in her head. 'Don't confide in her, Bell. Don't give me away to *her*!'

Bella managed a watery smile.

'I'm fine,' she said.

Mrs Parker's foot slid through the door. She was wearing her slippers, the ones shaped like rabbits with long furry ears that flopped back against her fat ankles.

'Been shopping for your Mum, have you?' she said, eyeing Bella's coat and the bulging carrier bag in the hall.

'Er – yes. We ran out of bread. Mo's still not well. I'm just… just going to make her a drink of lemon and honey.'

Mrs Parker leaned in between the closing door and the doorpost. Bella could not shut it any further without cracking her head like an egg.

'Blessed house has a chill on it like the grave,' muttered the woman. 'Let me come in and see…'

'No!' exclaimed Bella, beyond patience. 'Mo doesn't want to see *any* body…'

Dusty curls quivering in the bitter draught, Mrs Parker withdrew. The wind blustered into the hall and setting her shoulder to the door Bella shoved it to. Then she locked and bolted it in case the telephone caller should, by any chance, be lurking somewhere outside.

The wind getting up. Getting the wind up.

Both phrases, thought Bella, fitted her situation

51

perfectly tonight. Unable to settle she had neither lit the fire nor eaten but had come to bed with a hot water bottle. She had hoped to sleep the miseries away but her brain was racing. As though watching a horror film, she saw Mo in one terrifying situation after another. And like accompanying music the gale howled over the rooftops or prowled among the backyards, rattling loose boards in the fences, clattering the lids off the dustbins.

'Come on, Gosling,' she heard Mo admonish her. 'You're letting that imagination of yours run away with you. Think positive! Think of something *lovely*…'

So Bella tried. She conjured up a vision of Mo arriving home. With Oliver. Eyes shining with love and laughter they stooped over her.

'What d'you think, Bell?' Mo whispered. 'Your father wanted so much to see you that he asked me to meet him. To spend a few days with him. And you'll never believe it! We've decided to try again!'

'You're right,' agreed Bella. 'I don't believe it!'

The idea was too nonsensical and the vision dissolved leaving the black night to crowd in again.

When at last she slept Bella dreamed that it was she, not Mo, who was lost. She was walking among tall, half demolished buildings in a town she did not know. Waterways and railway lines constantly cut across her path so that it was as if she was wandering in a maze. From a signal box as big as County Hall, a policeman looked down at her.

'Into CARE!' he shouted. 'Or ELSE!'

As she turned to run she caught a glimpse of Mo. She was standing on the far side of a wooden gate calling, 'Bella – where are you Bella?'

'Here I am,' said Bella.

But Mo did not seem able to see her. Over and over again she shouted, 'Bella! Bella!,' and she started to kick and batter at the gate.

Coming up from sleep was like fighting her way to the surface of a treacle well. Bella was gasping for air and there was a sweet, sticky taste in her mouth.

Bella! Bang! Bella! Thump!

The house shuddered under the blows being struck on the front door. Her eyes gluey with sleep, Bella felt her way along the landing and down the stairs. As her damp fingers slithered over the key and slipped on the bolt she heard herself sobbing Mo's name. At last the door gave. The wind pounced at her and raindrops danced on the pavement. But she could not see anyone there.

Stepping out to look she felt the cold drench of rain through her pyjamas. From the park she heard the roar of the wind in the trees and the creak of the swings. And then, from the alleyway, the sound of thudding footsteps. Sharply she drew back.

'I thought you was never goin' to wake up!' gasped Matty, hurtling towards her.

Disappointment mingled with relief. Seizing the boy by his soaking anorak, Bella yanked him into the hall. Standing there, staring at each other but shivering too much to speak, they heard the living room clock chime two.

Chapter 12

One of Mo's luxuries was always to have plenty of hot water. The best way to warm Matty up, thought Bella, was to let him have a bath. While he got on with it she fetched

53

the small electric fire from Mo's bedroom and sat hunched over it in the living room.

This time, she thought, *I'm going to find out* all *about him.*

Half an hour later, when he came down, he was a changed child.

Changed child. Changeling.

He was wearing a pair of her pyjamas and a long cardigan of Mo's. His skull was smudged with old bruises and in the nape of his neck a single lock of uncut hair shone red gold in the light.

'I'm starvin',' he said.

Bella, who was also hungry, remembered the bargain they had struck last time.

'We'll eat,' she said, 'if you promise to tell me *every*thing…'

Matty squirmed. He could not possibly tell her everything. It would take all night and besides some of it was beyond telling.

'Please,' urged Bella. 'You've not told me anything, really, about yourself. Not even your name.'

'I have,' he protested. 'You calls me by it.' She was the only one, though, who had ever shortened his name to Matty and he liked that. It was something special between them.

'But Matthew what?'

'Byrd,' he said, dropping down beside her. 'Matthew Byrd.'

In Bella's weary brain things clicked and whirred. Matty who was watching her closely saw her flush and her eyes widen. She had the sort of face that showed everything she was feeling. It changed constantly. Sometimes she was quite plain, sometimes beautiful. He found this fascinating and felt he could never get tired of looking at her.

'Were you around the park all day today?' she asked.

'Mostly.'

'And did anyone know that?'

'Mebbe. The Gang've been doggin' me for days.'

'Then it must have been *you* they wanted,' murmured Bella. 'Not me!' And she told him about the telephone call outside St Barnabas' church hall. 'I thought they were *real* gangsters,' she said, 'who'd kidnapped Mo!'

'Nope. It'd be me they wanted awright! They knows I'd answer the 'phone, see.'

'Why?'

'I allus does.'

It was a joke at Elmbridge House. Everybody knew he could not resist a ringing telephone, no matter where he was. He had done it once in the Headmaster's office at school. It would not have been so bad but the Head was actually there at the time, grilling him about one of his absences…

He sniggered at the memory and Bella's eyes flashed.

'You're not listening to me,' she said. 'I just asked you what *is* this Gang? Who are the boys and why are they after you? I mean — what do they want?'

She was firing questions at him like adults so often did, not giving him time to think, much less answer. He realised he was going to have to give her some information.

'George and Arnie's from the Home,' he said quickly. 'They're the worst. The others are their mates from school.'

'Bullies!' she exclaimed.

Matty shrugged. At Elmbridge House bullying was just a fact of life. George and Arnie bullied everyone. All of them were in care – but nobody in the world *seemed* to care. None of their families did for sure. As for the official carers some of them weren't above a bit of rough stuff either. A sneaky pinch here, a sharp prod there, a shake (in quiet corners) that nearly took your head off.

'George and Arnie takes me money, see,' he said. 'Me pocket money, that is. *And* the fivers me Gran sometimes sends. They're mad with me now 'cos I found where George hides it – and pinched it back!'

'On the 'phone they said that if you didn't give them what they wanted by tomorrow, they'd do something awful.'

Matty snuffled with laughter.

'Tryin' to skeer me!' he said.

'Well they sure as anything scared me!' Bella was outraged.

'What they really wants,' said Matty, 'is me snow ball. Even more than the money.'

He remembered George's face when Arnie, holding the snow globe out of Matty's reach, had shown it to him.

'That's worth summat, that is!' George had said, impressed. 'An antique like that! Could sell that for *real* dosh, Arn. Plenty o' fags – and the rest – in that!'

With a great leap, Matty had snatched it out of Arnie's grasp and run. Only his cunning and his agility had kept it from them since.

'So that's what the 'phone call was all about,' marvelled Bella. 'The snow globe.'

Matty's stomach rumbled loudly and giving it a thump he jumped off the settee. 'When we goin' to eat?' he demanded.

By three o'clock they were tucking into another of

Matty's meals. He'd found prawns and chicken nuggets in the freezing compartment of the fridge and fried them up with thick slices of Bella's new bread and a couple of squashy tomatoes. They finished off with chocolate icecream sprinkled with hundreds and thousands and mugs of orange fizz.

'That's the best midnight feast I've ever had,' sighed Bella.

She'd had midnight feasts with Ali when Ali slept over at Number 21. Sometimes Mo, complaining that they kept her awake with their giggling, came in to join them. But really that spoiled it.

Now her eyelids felt hot and heavy and a yawn ached in her throat.

'You know,' she said sleepily. 'I thought that 'phone call was for me because *I'm* called Birdie too.'

Matty bounced up and down so that his fork shot off his plate and clattered against the electric fire. Wrapping one arm around his neck he held himself in a headlock.

'Cor!' he shouted. 'Cool! *Both* Birdie! That's a sign that is! It's another… another proper sign!'

Chapter 13

Matty had lived with his grandmother until he was eight and it was from her that he had picked up his feeling for signs. *She* believed in them absolutely.

'They're like fingerposts, Matt,' she said. 'Pointin' your way through the world.'

Her faith in them began on the day when she first saw his grandfather. 'I were no more'n a slip of a girl,' she told Matty. 'And he were a ganglin', out-at-elbows lad.'

She lived in the village near Tamarton where she still lived and – with a group of other wartime evacuees – he had come there from London. He was boarded with the Nethercotts who had the big farm on the western edge of the moor.

'The night afore I first set eyes on 'n,' she said, 'I dreamed about a boy on a white horse. Black haired and 'ansome he were as he come ridin' toward me out o' the mist. Then lo and behold, the very next mornin', there were Joe, perched on the back of Jan Nethercott's grey shire mare. There were a sea fret mufflin' everythin' that mornin' but all on a sudden the sun peeped through. It beamed on to Joe's black hair so it shone blue as a rook's wing. I could tell he were half excited, half afeerd to be on that blessed great horse. But he looked me boldly in the eye and winked! I knowed then as I'd marry un!'

She laughed and her sad eyes brightened. Then she went on to tell other, darker stories, about other signs.

Long before Matty was taken and put into care she knew he was going to leave. In dreams she saw him walking away from her, dwindling into the distance. And she kept losing things; photographs of him as a baby, a stone he had once painted at school, a pottery rabbit he had won at a fair and given her as a present. She assured Matty that he had this same gift of recognising signs and on the day she gave him the snow globe he knew she was right.

The globe had been lying in the dust at the back of her cupboard, waiting for him, its meaning hidden until he and he alone learned to 'read' it. As he was shunted from Home to foster home and back his faith in it never wavered. Together with his belief in himself it helped him to survive. He never showed it to anyone else but often, when on his own, he brooded over it. For the scene inside it was so precise and yet so changeable, that surely it was magic!

Sometimes the light inside it was warm, golden, sunny. Sometimes cool and colourless. Sometimes green and lowering as if a storm were about to break. When he shook the snow the branches of the tree appeared to toss and sway as if stirred by the wind. And afterwards, as the flakes settled, the shape and position of everything seemed to have shifted slightly...

It had been a long time before he discovered that if he squinted through the flaws in the glass he saw things magnified. And noticed things he hadn't seen at all before. He spent hours puzzling over the tree and the creatures in the tree but from the beginning what enthralled him most was the girl. The glow of her hair. The dancing swing of her green coat. The way her face was turned aside so you couldn't see it fully and had to guess her eyes were green. Like his own.

The girl bewitched him.

So, two weeks ago, in Old Meadow Park, when Bella had flown to his rescue, long coat swishing about her ankles, green eyes blazing, hair aflame, he knew at once that he had found her.

And from then on he knew where he was going.

Chapter 14

Shortly after six o'clock, Bella was woken by the sound of someone retching in the bathroom. Fuzzy with sleep, she sat up.

'Mo?' she called. 'Are you all right?'

59

Rolling out of bed she went to see and found Matty hanging over the lavatory bowl. With an exclamation of sympathy (of all things in the world she hated being sick) Bella put one arm round him and placed her other hand on his forehead. The way Mo always did for her. He turned to look at her, his eyes bleary and bloodshot.

'Must've been those prawns, I reckon,' he said.

'The funny mixture more likely,' said Bella.

But *she* felt all right. She wondered if Matty were starting with chicken pox. He felt very hot and sweat glistened on the shiny skin beneath the faint golden down of his hair.

Slowly he relaxed against her and the urge to throw up died down. Not since he had been taken from his Gran had anyone held him, close and comforting, like that.

When he was sure it was over, they went downstairs again and Bella wrapped him in the blanket she had found for him earlier. Switching on the electric fire she turned over his damp clothes which had been drying in front of it.

Outside the wind had quietened and the rain stopped. The only sounds now were the tick of the clock and the drip drip of water leaking from the broken gutter on the front of the house.

'You got so wet and cold,' Bella said, sitting back beside him. 'Were you wandering about all night before you came here?'

'No,' he said. 'I were kippin' in the boneyard.'

'What?!'

Matty grinned. He and Bella spoke different languages. But whereas he understood hers he saw she was often puzzled by his.

'The cemetery,' he explained.

Boneyard was his Gran's word. She spoke a different language too, one that was rooted in the past and the place from which she came. The way he spoke, however, was mainly of his own making. In the early days at Elmbridge House he had been picked on for his country speech and for his occasional use of long words. So he had worked hard on it, shaping it to match the speech of those around him.

'The one over the park,' he went on. 'I been there before. There's a tomb like a flat stone bed, see. It's all covered over with trees and secrety. The Gang'd never think of lookin' for me there.'

'I should think not,' she shuddered. 'Among all those dead bodies! Spooky!'

But Matty had not been spooked. The dead could not hurt you.

'It's a good place for sleepin',' he joked. 'That's what they're all doin' in there!' Carved in the stone where he had curled up were the words 'Rest in Peace'. 'I did rest in peace an' all,' he said. 'Till the rain come down in barrel loads!'

He leaned back and closed his eyes. The electric fire hummed and steam rose from his drying clothes. There was a faint smell of scorching. Bella studied his face. It was white and pinched looking with the cut on his cheek a dark, scabbed scar.

But when he's awake, she thought, his face lights up. And there's always a sort of sly laughter lurking in his eyes.

Reaching across him she picked up his rucksack, meaning to put it on the floor out of his way. At once his eyes opened and he made a grab for it.

'Mind me snow ball,' he said.

He set the bag on his lap and lifted out the globe, cradling it to him as if it were a cuddly teddy bear instead of a cold, glass sphere. On the night before They had come to take him into Care, he had nagged at his Gran to let him take it with him. She had complained that he would 'weasel the very blood out o' my veins,' but then she had wrapped it in tissue paper and thrust it into his hands.

'Look after it, Matt,' she said. ''Tis main precious. My Da carried it all the way back from France in 1945. Spoils of war, he said. But I reckon 't was the spoils of a love affair he had over there…'

And she had shaken with silent laughter.

Now Bella touched it lightly with one finger and asked if she could hold it for a minute. He opened his hands. The glow from the electric bars filled the globe with a crimson light like a frosty winter sunset. Against this the tree's branches spread in a black web. And at its roots, piled high about the girl's skirts, the snow glittered.

Imprisoning her, thought Bella, her eye to the flaw. And the cold is creeping up towards her heart. With a shiver she said, 'It's odd. The girl really does look like me. But I don't see what that has to do with destiny? It's just an accident…'

Yet destiny, she supposed, was shaped by events which seemed to be accidents. Like Mo becoming pregnant with Bella. Like Matty's Gran being suddenly unable to cope. Like Mo going missing… and Matty turning up…

Matty gave a little snore and slumped sideways. He was different from any other boy she knew. Less cocky – but underneath more truly sure of himself. Although his rough speech could not express it well, she sensed a kind of wisdom in him. An acceptance of things as they were

62

alongside a quiet determination to change them. He seemed both older and younger than he was.

Replacing the snow globe carefully in his rucksack, she lifted his legs so that he could lie straight. Then switching off the fire she crept upstairs to bed.

THURSDAY

Bella overslept and it was nearly breaktime when she set off for school. She might not have gone at all except that Matty insisted.

'You got to behave like normal,' he said, spreading egg and mayonnaise on her sandwiches for lunch. 'If you don't, you knows what'll happen. Care!'

The way he said it the word 'care' sounded like 'death'.

'Well, don't you answer the door to anyone,' she advised.

She was nervous about Nosy Parker. Or worse still, Mrs Jenkins. But she felt like one of the Seven Dwarfs warning Snow White about the Wicked Queen.

'What if your Mam comes home?' he asked.

Bella frowned, thinking it a silly question. If only Mo would! Then she laughed as she tried to imagine Mo's face if she let herself into the house and was confronted by a strange boy with no hair and wearing a pair of Bella's outgrown, pink dungarees.

At school she explained she was late because Mo was in bed with chicken pox.

Under her straight, black fringe Miss Fairfax's eyes were troubled.

'I thought something wasn't quite right this week, Bella,' she said. 'You've been unlike yourself. Dreamy. And tired. Are you managing all right?'

Again Bella lurched towards confession but thinking of Matty she pressed her lips tightly together. Later she was glad she had said nothing.

'What's this?' demanded Miss Fairfax with her sharp pencil poised above Bella's English book. 'It looks as though a centipede with inky feet has crawled across the page. Usually your work is neat – at least!'

Crossly Bella doodled words in the margin.

Brilliant, she wrote. Scintillating. Inspired. Fantastic.

Then, in tiny letters underneath, she printed, 'At least,' and underlined it several times.

By the time she was on her way home, Bella's head felt very odd. As if it might float off her shoulders any minute and sail away over the rooftops. Like those shiny helium filled balloons they sold in Orbury at Christmas time.

Once, when she was small, Mo had bought her one of these balloons and afterwards had taken her into the Cathedral to see the Crib. In the doorway the Bishop himself had been talking to the Verger. There was a flutter of raised hands, a wink of anxious light on spectacles.

'Madam,' tutted the Bishop, stooping over Bella. 'Think of the consequences if the child should let it go!' And he pointed to the fan vaulting which soared high above their heads like the canopy of a stone forest. Flushing, but giggling too, Mo tied the balloon string securely round Bella's wrist.

'I suppose it would look bad,' she said. 'Batman grinning down from among all those stony-faced angels!'

Wherever Mo goes, thought Bella, she seems to walk slap into trouble…

Looking up she saw she was already back in Old Meadow Park. Ahead of her, under Matty's chestnut tree, four boys slouched. In jeans and anoraks, their dark hair cropped close, they leaned together, talking, smoking. The sun, glaring from the edge of a cloud, caught them full in its light and one of them glanced furtively over his shoulder.

Bella slowed down and pretended to watch the children playing on the slide. She was fairly sure these boys were 'the Gang'. Were they waiting now for Matty to turn up? Thinking about yesterday's telephone call she remembered uneasily that they had given him just twenty-four hours.

None of them was looking her way so she left the play area and started to cross the road.

'Hey! You there! Gingernob!'

Raising her head a little higher she kept going.

'Hang on, hang on,' called another voice. 'We want a word with you, Carrots!'

She was midway between the park and Number 21. What if Matty saw her and came to the door? Bella hesitated. Half turned back.

'What d'you want?' she asked innocently.

'We wants Birdie,' said the one who'd spoken first.

'Yeah! The little runt wiv the bald head!'

'Don't know him,' said Bella.

'Oh yeah you do. 'E was the one wiv us the ovver day. The day your big sister come out of the 'ouse over there... screetin' and scratchin' like a wild cat!'

They all laughed, a coarse, discordant sound. Yet they looked harmless. Clean and respectable. And the one who'd called her Carrots – she had a feeling it was Arnie – was actually rather dishy.

''E's a villain, our Birdie is. 'E's run away from 'ome and 'e's been seen lurkin' about this park...'

The boy leered at her and another one said, 'His Mum's half daft with worry.'

'And 'is Dad!'

'Well if he's run away, why would he come here?' shrugged Bella. 'There's nowhere to hide in this park and

69

nothing whatsoever to eat!'

Even as she said this Bella thought it sounded silly. But she was playing for time. Wanting to put the Gang off the scent but not sure how. She had a feeling they knew very well that she knew something about Matty. And sure enough the good-looking boy stepped closer to her, blue eyes hard and unblinking.

'I think you do know something, though,' he said quietly.

Bella shook her head but inside her warm coat, she shivered as he continued to stare at her. *Yes*, she thought, *I'm sure he's Arnie.*

Out of the corner of her eye she saw Mrs Parker come out on to her doorstep with an empty milk bottle in her hand. Turning away from the boy she called and waved. Mrs Parker looked surprised but waved back.

'I've got to go,' said Bella. 'I'm supposed to be having my tea with her today.' As if answering Bella's silent prayer Mrs Parker did not go back inside but came down the step and stood on the footpath as though waiting for her. The boy retreated a little.

'You go then, Freckleface,' he said. 'But we'll be keeping an eye on you.'

'Yeah,' said one of the others. 'There's fings the *police* might like to know about you! Know what I mean?'

'You're crazy,' said Bella breezily. But her heart was stuttering in her chest and her head felt ready to lift off.

Arnie breathed a stream of blue smoke into her face and she swung away from him, marching defiantly to where Mrs Parker still waited. Behind her she heard the boys snigger and jeer. In front of her Mrs Parker watched her approach with a greedily inquisitive expression.

Chapter 16

'She thought I was larking about with them,' Bella said to Matty an hour later. '*Flirting!*' She wrinkled her nose in disgust. 'So I told her they were being horrible to me and pretended to be upset. Then she insisted on taking me into her house and I had to fend off all her questions about Mo!'

A little flare of anger spurted in her again at the thought of Mo's desertion. She slammed a cake tin down on the table.

'Nosy Parker's kind in some ways, I suppose,' she sighed. 'She gave me this cake and said if there was anything she could do I only had to ask...'

Matty stirred lumps of butter into the pasta he had just drained. He had raided Mo's stores and found a tin of tomatoes, one onion, two shrivelled cloves of garlic and the last of the cheese. From this he had made a rich sauce which he now ladled over the pasta.

'You're a wicked cook,' Bella said, dipping her finger into the bowl he gave her.

'Me Gran taught me,' said Matty. 'She couldn't do much, see, because of her arthur...'

'Her Arthur?'

'Ritis. Her arthur-ritis.'

Leading the way into the living room he thought of the time when he was very small, before the pain had locked all his Gran's joints. She'd been quite sprightly then. And she was always a good cook. He remembered one summer's day when heat hazed the distant hills and she'd packed up a picnic of homemade chicken pie and his favourite lemon cake. They'd taken a bus in Tamarton and gone out into the country.

'Where we goin,' Gran?' he'd asked.

'Wait and you'll see,' she replied.

The funny thing was he could not recall much about the rest of the day. Except there was a house like a castle and gardens so big you could get lost in them. They'd sat by a stream and watched a dragonfly, blue as a shred of sky, hover above the water while she'd told him how *her* mother had once worked in this place...

'Hey,' said Bella. 'Are you going to stand there for ever staring into space or are you going to come and eat?'

She lowered herself on to the hearthrug and began to fork up the pasta. Firelight played on her face, warming its pallor.

'I don't think the Gang actually know you're here,' she said. 'Not yet anyway.'

Matty flopped down beside her. 'They ent very clever,' he said.

Bella was not so sure. Fetching Mrs Parker's cake she cut two wedges of sticky chocolate sponge.

'I guess I should have told her the truth about Mo,' she said.

Misery threatened to overwhelm her. Sinking her teeth into the cake which was very good, she said, on impulse, 'D'you want to see my Dad?'

Matty's hand froze half way to his lips.

'You said you ent got a Dad,' he protested.

Bella shuffled across to the television and switched it on. A game show nattered at them from the screen. She leaned back against the settee. Matty finished his cake, cut himself another piece, and waited patiently.

The game show ended and the commercials began. The camera panned across a wide view of English countryside. Golden wheatfields shining in the sun.

Beside him Matty felt Bella stiffen. Then a thin, dark man appeared, beating eggs in a blue and white bowl.

That's him, he thought.

I shouldn't have said, thought Bella. *I don't want to share Oliver with anybody. He's my secretest secret…*

Abruptly she leaned over and turned the picture off. She made no comment but sat in silence with shoulders bowed.

Sensing it was no use asking questions, Matty suggested they should play cards. Reluctantly she agreed and found a pack. They played Snap and Rummy and Strip Jack Naked. With each game Matty kept winning and Bella grew more and more bad-tempered.

'Snarlygogs!' she swore, throwing the pack down. 'I don't feel like playing these stupid games!'

The lost night's sleep had long ago caught up with her.

'I can't go on like this,' she wailed. 'I'll have to tell *someone* about Mo! She's never done this to me before. What if she's hurt… in danger. …and I've done *nothing…*'

The words trailed away and Matty saw tears glinting on her cheeks. Although he did not do too well at school (he was not often there) he knew a lot about people. He was so used to them letting him down that Mo's disappearance did not surprise him. But he understood that it was different for Bella, that her mother's unexplained absence was making her frightened, confused and unhappy.

He did not know how to express his understanding to her so he juggled with the cards, shuffling them expertly before making them spring in a smooth arc from one hand to the other. Intrigued and distracted for a moment, Bella watched as he brought the whole pack together and then, pretending to be puzzled, plucked the Knave of Hearts from behind her ear and the Joker from his own sock.

'Who taught you to do that?' she asked.

'Me first foster Dad,' he said. 'Dave.'

He had liked Dave. He was nearer to being a proper father than anyone else who had cared for him.

'Why didn't you stay with him?' asked Bella.

Matty shrugged. 'There were trouble with Meg,' he said. 'That's his wife. He got too deep into computers, see. First it were the games, then it were the Internet. Spent all his spare time – and his money – on it and she couldn't stand it...'

He stopped, hearing again the rows that went on late into the night. Meg shrieking that Dave no longer cared, that she might as well have *married* a computer...

'She pushed off,' he said. 'And never came back.'

'Like Mo,' murmured Bella.

She pressed her fingers against her eyelids, forcing back the tears that threatened again.

'Oh!' she cried. 'Who can I *tell* about Mo?'

Matty frowned down at the cards in his hand. Their garish, expressionless faces seemed to mock him but somewhere at the back of his mind a startling new idea stirred.

Chapter 17

Matty dreamed about his grandmother. She was not in her own tiny cottage but was standing beneath the high dome of a room whose walls and ceiling glittered as if they were carved from the inside of an iceberg. His Gran was too far away for him to see her clearly but he knew her by the curve of her back as she stooped over her two walking sticks.

'Boy!' she shouted, raising one stick and shaking it at him. 'Have you taken your dirty boots off?'

Looking down at his feet he saw they were naked and rooted in the ice.

'Watch out for the signs, Matt,' cried his Gran. 'You must keep a watch for the signs!'

He tried to move towards her but could not budge because of his trapped feet. Around him the sparkling room was creaking and crackling as if it were beginning to split apart.

With a shout he awoke. His heart was hammering high in his chest and his feet were icy cold. He groped for his blanket and found it had slithered to the floor. In his head he could still hear the echoes of his grandmother's voice.

'I did watch out for the signs, Gran,' he said. 'I *do!*'

Closing his eyes he saw her face in the darkness behind them. Her skin like crumpled tissue paper. Her hair straggling out of its bun. Her blue eyes clouded with pain.

'Hold fast to your dreams, Matt,' she whispered. 'Don't 'ee let 'n go.'

Wrapping the blanket more closely round him, Matty considered these words. What he dreamed of was belonging. As he had belonged once with his Gran (only they had taken him away from her) and as he had wanted to belong with Dave (only Dave had let him down). Since then he had spent much of his time on the run.

Unless you lived with people who loved and needed you as much as you loved and needed them there was nothing to hold you. So whenever things got too much, when he felt if he did not go he would break out and smash the place up or take it out of someone smaller – as George and Arnie did – he took off. But although it gave him a sense of freedom, of being in charge of his own life, running away never led anywhere. Except back to Elmbridge House. Or to scary, lonely nights in some distant, vast, uncaring city.

Now, however, it was different. He had met Bella and he felt that he and his dreams were back on track.

'Ent no good, though,' he muttered to himself, 'if her Mam don't come home.'

He pondered over the idea the cards had suggested to him but shook his head despondently.

'That ent a proper sign,' he said. 'What I wants is a *proper* sign.'

Taking the snow globe from its paper bag in his rucksack, he held it close to his face. In the frail light which leaked through the curtains from the street lamp, he could just see the black tracery of the tree's branches, the glimmer of the snow, the smudge of the girl's coat. Half asleep he sat there blinking and murmuring to himself, while outside the Pavilion Street cats went wailing and caterwauling through the park.

FRIDAY

Chapter 18

The first thing Bella remembered when she woke up was that she needed money. She had run out of pocket money, there was no bread in the house and Friday was the morning the milkman called to be paid.

Shrugging on her dressing gown, she left her own small room at the back of the house and went into Mo's. The bedside clock told her it was seven-thirty. Tiptoeing about so that she did not wake Matty down below, she began to search.

Mo was like a squirrel. She hid small sums of money – 'For rainy days, Gosling' – in odd places all over the house. Bella sometimes found a pound coin inside some hollow ornament and once she had discovered a five pound note under the plasters in the first aid tin. Now she shook every pot and lifted every jar on Mo's dressing table. There was nothing. From among the tangle of beads and bangles in the jewellery box she sorted a twenty pence piece, three French coins and an old penny.

'I swear,' she grunted, as she tipped them back, 'when I grow up I'll be as different from Mo as possible. To start with I'll get myself a proper education!'

Mo's education had been cut short by Bella's birth. Since then, whenever she could afford it, she had been to evening classes: painting and pottery, French and poetry, yoga and drama.

'Bits of this and bobs of that, Bell! A rag-bag of skills for a rag-bag of a person!'

But Mo was not a rag-bag. She was clever, quick to learn and everything she did showed flair. What she lacked was steadiness!

Mo's beautiful too, thought Bella, catching sight of

herself in the mirror. So why am I plain?

In her head she heard her mother's husky laugh.

'It's just a stage you're going through, Gosling! The stage when nothing quite seems to *match*. In a year or two you'll be fine…'

But how could she ever be fine if Mo never came back!

For all her fecklessness Mo always seemed to know what to do when disasters loomed. Now, facing the worst disaster of her life, Bella herself felt lost, trapped in a labyrinth where every idea she followed came at last to a dead end.

Beside the mirror a clay bust of her grandfather stared at her, his eyes blank and blind under jutting eyebrows.

'You were no better,' she reproved him. 'You ran away too!'

The bust was one of Mo's pottery rejects and for a joke she had covered its baldness with a wig of black curls she had worn when she played a gypsy girl in some long ago play. Bella plucked the wig off her grandfather and pulled it over her own fiery curls. In the dawn light it made her look paler than ever. Twisting this way and that she tried to see some likeness to her dark haired father. But Oliver's hair was cropped short, his skin tanned a healthy brown.

Tearing the wig off she tossed it back on to her grandfather where it slipped over one eye, making him look drunk – or demented.

From downstairs she thought she heard the sound of movement and paused to listen. But the house was silent. Instead, amid the roar of early morning traffic on Upper Park Road, she heard the whine of an electric milk float. Quickly she crossed to her mother's wardrobe and started to rake through it. She found a heap of Mo's shoes and a box of old postcards but even Mo's pockets yielded only a beermat, two odd earrings and the wrapper off a chocolate bar.

Had Mo ransacked the house for money before leaving?

Deciding she would have to search the living room too, Bella went down.

'Matty,' she whispered at the door.

There was no answer so she crept inside. In spite of the gloom behind the drawn curtains she saw at once that the couch was empty, the blanket neatly folded over its back. Racing into the kitchen she peered into the yard and then pounded upstairs to the bathroom. But Matty was nowhere.

'Gog and Snarlygog,' she cried, returning to the living room. 'Why does *everyone* desert me! And why on earth would Matty run away from *here*!'

Chapter 19

The solid world seemed to quiver and quake. Like Alice when she drank the magic potion, Bella felt herself shrinking while everything around her grew monstrously large and threatening. In the last twenty-four hours only Matty had stood between her and panic.

Trying to fight it off she attacked the room. She tossed Mo's precious ornaments about. She dragged the Indian cover off the settee and swept the sewing from the table. She punched the cushions and flung them on the floor. She pulled the books down from the shelves and shook each one. Papers fluttered out of them: recipes, receipts, names and addresses, unfinished poems, foreign stamps, one old pound note and a newspaper clipping.

83

The clipping yellow with age, dropped on her bare feet and unfolded.

ACTOR TAKES POETRY SHOW ON TOUR, said the headline.

Bella picked it up. Across the fold, creased and faded, there was the grainy photograph of a man. Although he was younger, his face more rounded and his black hair hanging in ringlets to his shoulders there was no mistaking Oliver's crooked smile. Straightening the paper she skimmed the first paragraph.

Oliver Montford, whose work as an actor is, he claims at best patchy, has a part-time post at Peverell College in Waterham where he teaches drama and theatre studies. With a group of his students he has devised an exciting show of music and poetry with which they are about to tour middle schools in the South West...

There were more details of the show but nothing more about Oliver. At the bottom, in the right hand margin, there were faint marks scratched with a pencil. Moving closer to the lamp, Bella squinted at them trying to decipher them. She had made nothing of them when someone rapped sharply on the front door, making her jump. The milkman!

Laying the paper aside she stared in a daze at the wreckage of the room. Yet she had not found a single penny! Her heart sinking she went into the hall. For how many weeks did Mo owe money? The door knocker banged again.

'My mother's ill,' she muttered as she tugged the door open. 'I spent the milk money on medicines...'

'Mornin' Missus!' said Matty, grinning at her from under his baseball cap.

Bella's hand shot out and she grabbed his arm. For a

84

second she hesitated, wondering whether to push or pull, then she hauled him off the step and slammed the door behind him.

'Where've you been?' she shouted.

He covered his ears with his hands because they were sensitive to loud noise. Always inclined to be hasty Bella was wound up to such a pitch that she thought he was deliberately trying to shut her out. Thrusting her face closer to his she shouted louder than ever.

'You should have told me you were going. I thought you'd done a runner again! Why did you go? You might have run slap, bang into one of the Gang out there!'

'What! Them!' muttered Matty, wondering what had got into her. 'You must be jokin'! You wouldn't catch any of them out of bed before breakfus'.'

'Well other people then,' she said stubbornly. 'The police... The people from Elmbridge House. *They* must be looking for you by now.'

Matty's eyes gleamed with derisive laughter.

'The police ent much good at catchin' me,' he said. 'I been on the run too often.'

The tip of his nose was red, a drip forming as he warmed up in the house. Wiping it on his sleeve he produced a carrier bag from behind his back.

'Food,' he said.

'You've been stealing!' Bella was truly shocked.

Matty was not offended at her suspicion. There had been plenty of times when he had taken food without paying for it. Rattling the change in his pocket he reminded her of the money he had recovered from George and Arnie.

'I paid 'cos I knowed you'd be sticky about it,' he said. Brushing past her he went into the kitchen and

85

unloaded the bag. Thick sliced bread, strawberry jam, eggs, a packet of cornflakes.

'You ent goin' to school hungry,' he said, echoing words his Gran had often said to him.

Moodily she leaned against the doorpost and watched him. Behind her the front door shuddered as someone else knocked on it. This time it *was* the milkman.

'Don't ee fret about the money, Maidy,' he said 'Us'll not starve this week. Give your pretty Mam my love – and hope she's better soon.'

His eyes slid together over the bridge of his nose and whistling cheerfully he returned to his float. Bella stayed on the step and looked up and down the street. It was very quiet. In the park the trees were knee deep in a milky fog. From behind the three poplars that stood like angels with folded wings over the graveyard, a white faced sun struggled to shine. Matty was right. So far there was no one about. No member of the Gang. No policeman.

From the kitchen she could hear the kettle singing and the smell of toast drifted out to her. Returning to the living room she drew back the curtains. The pale daylight washed over the newspaper cutting she had left on the table. Bella looked at it and looked again. For now she could clearly see the pencilling in the margin. It was a name and address.

Monty, it said in Mo's neat handwriting. *Guinevere's Bower. Owlcombe. Near Waterham.*

Chapter 20

Matty could scarcely believe it. It was the sign he had been wanting. And it seemed all the more powerful because it reinforced the idea which had occurred to him the night before. The idea which had then seemed too daring, too scary.

Wallowing elbow deep in sudsy washing-up water he said so to Bella.

'You and your signs,' she scoffed. 'I don't believe in signs!'

Matty tipped bubbles from one mug into another. He knew he would have to tread carefully.

'It's like this,' he said. 'You've lost your Mam and there ent *no one* you can tell is there?'

Bella was silent. She hated that word, 'lost'. It had such a final sound.

'Then,' Matty went on, 'just when you're gettin' desperate, you happens on this address – and there your Dad is. As if it's *meant*, see!'

She shook her head. *Dad, Oliver, Monty*, she thought. Three different names for nobody. He was merely a dream in her head, an image flickering on a screen, a name in a long ago newspaper.

'Forget it!' she said. 'It's a stupid idea. Why should *he* do anything to help? I frightened him off even before I was born!'

Matty wiped his hands on his jeans.

'If I knowed where my Dad was,' he said, 'I'd go…'

He stopped because he was not sure that was the truth. He had one happy memory of his father. In others he figured as an angry, loud-voiced giant. Someone of whom he had been half afraid. All the same he thought that Bella should trust her dreams. Dreams, like signs, helped you to find your way through life. Without them you were like a stick thrown into a stream, carried wherever the current took you, with no notion of where you wanted to go.

'Guinevere's Bower,' he said softly. 'It's a pretty name, ent it?'

At once Bella could see it. A round stone tower with a winding stair. Sunlight falling aslant arched windows. A path edged with hollyhocks. Swallows swooping around the high eaves…

But not in the middle of winter! And the idea of going to find Oliver was ridiculous.

'It's no good,' she said. 'I couldn't possibly. Anyway Waterham's miles away – and I've no money.'

'I has though,' said Matty.

Upstairs Bella was making a great racket, opening and shutting drawers. Matty packed sandwiches into his rucksack and took out his snow globe. Shaking it he whisked the snow into a blizzard. Thicker and thicker it spiralled around the tree and the girl until all he could see of them was a single dark shadow. Then, impatient to be off, he dropped it back into his bag and dashed to the door, almost knocking Bella over as she entered the room, her arms laden with clothes.

'What they for?' he asked. 'We ent goin' on holiday!'

'Arnie's out there. Under the chestnut tree. I saw him from Mo's room.'

'That don't matter,' said Matty, hopping about. 'We'll go out over the back wall.'

'Yes. But we have to go into Orbury and there'll be other people looking for you by now. You've been away from the Home for days!'

Spreading the clothes out across the back of the settee she said, 'I don't want to be with you when they catch you. Think of the trouble *I'd* be in! You've got to disguise yourself…'

Matty wanted to laugh but saw she was deadly serious. 'Awright,' he shrugged. 'I reckon it'll be a lark, dressin' up!'

Rapidly sorting through the clothes he settled on Bella's pink dungarees again, with a white sweater and her old blue anorak.

'But what are we going to do about your head?' she moaned. 'You can't wear your cap, it's too distinctive. And no one could miss your bald head!'

He ran his hand over his scalp and felt the prickle of the new hair growing.

'What I needs,' he joked, 'is a wig.'

'Done!' said Bella. And she fetched Mo's gypsy curls.

Matty's green eyes sparked with indignation and he fought her off as she tried to force the wig on to his head. 'I ent wearing' *that*,' he shouted.

Bella backed away and stood with it wrapped round her hands like a muff. 'It's either this,' she said. 'Or I don't go.'

He could see she was as tense and concentrated as an acrobat on a high wire. Any opposition and she would flip. She was not used to dangerous living as he was. He took the wig and pulled it on.

'That's ace!' she exclaimed. 'Even your Gran wouldn't know you. It makes you look like a girl.'

Matty was horrified.

Though if I had of been a girl, he thought, *me Gran might of coped better.*

89

He was mincing round the room in mockery of a girl's walk when there was a soft thump on the front door and the letter box snapped open. They both ran into the hall. Lying on the mat was a grubby piece of paper torn out of a school exercise book. Bella picked it up.

WE KNOW BIRDIES IN THERE, she read. IF HE DONT COME OUT TO THE PARK INSIDE AN HOUR AND GIVE US <u>YOU KNOW WHAT</u> WE'RE PHONING THE POLICE

'See!' she said. 'I told you!'

Matty grinned and shouldered his rucksack.

'Well,' he said. 'I reckons we *got* to go now – ent we?'

Chapter 21

The only bus going from Orbury to Waterham that day, had left two hours ago. Undaunted Matty led the way through the busy streets down to the train station. All the way they argued about whether he should pay for his ticket or not.

'I allus goes free,' he insisted.

'But how?' asked Bella who was scandalised but intrigued.

Matty shrugged. 'Usually I hides in the toilet when the ticket man comes round.'

One of his carers, taking him to a new foster home, had taught him the trick of it. You had to have your wits about you but it worked. When on the run he had travelled miles like that.

'No,' said Bella. 'Not this time. Not when you're with me.'

Grumbling Matty bought two tickets.

There was an hour to wait for the train. They went into the buffet and had a hot chocolate but Bella could not settle. She was nervous and restless. There were so many alarming 'what ifs' ahead of them.

Out on the platform, pigeons fluttered under the roof and bobbed around their feet. Matty lunged to catch one and his wig slid forward over his eyes. Both of them spluttered with laughter. A muffled, crackly voice announced the arrival of the train.

The carriage was crowded and they sat squashed together opposite a gaunt, worried-looking woman who kept trying to talk to her husband who only grunted from behind his newspaper. Matty sat hugging his bag, watching other people, wondering where each of them was going and why. Bella gazed out of the window.

Gradually the land flattened out into wide green spaces intersected by canals where pollarded willows, like knobbly heads with hair standing on end, leaned over the water. A fox, loping across a field, stopped and turned to look at the train. Across the misty distance its eyes seemed to meet Bella's. Almost as if it knew what she was up to.

'You might get there. You'll never get there,' chuntered the train. 'You might get there. You'll never get there.'

'I'm starvin',' said Matty. 'Let's eat.'

So they ate strawberry jam sandwiches and crackers wedged together with expensive tinned pate which Matty had found at the back of Mo's store cupboard.

By the time they were running among hills again it seemed already to be growing dark. The train lights came on and the man with the newspaper snored loudly. Bella searched for the map she had put in her duffle bag. Slipped inside it – for Oliver – was a black and white photograph of Mo taken before Bella was born. Instead of the boyish bob she now wore, her hair streamed over her shoulders in a shining cape. She looked unusually solemn.

Matty liked maps. Ever since he could remember he had enjoyed studying them and once, at school, he had won a gold star for drawing one. Now he pored over this one, completely absorbed, until Bella nudged him. 'How far is it from Waterham to where... to the village where... to Owlcombe...?' she asked.

'About ten miles,' he said.

'What!'

''S awright,' he assured her. 'There'll be a bus.'

He felt warm and full and contented. He enjoyed travelling. What's more each extra mile took him farther from the Gang, and from Elmbridge House. Even if they did not find Oliver the journey was an adventure in itself. On journeys you never quite knew what would happen next...

Chapter 22

'Sorry, girls,' said a cheerful driver in Waterham bus station. 'No bus to Owlcombe before four o'clock. You'd be better catching the Stretton bus and walking.'

'Girls!?'

Matty had had enough of disguise. As soon as the driver turned his back he plucked off the wig and pushed it into his rucksack. The cold air struck his naked head like a blow. It felt as if it came straight from the Arctic. And above the hills that surrounded the city the cloudy sky had a strange sepia tint, like the colour of the sky in an old photograph.

It's going to snow, he thought. But he kept that thought to himself.

When they jumped off the bus in Stretton, Bella's stomach did a slow, sickening somersault. They were within walking distance of Oliver, the nearest she had ever been to her father. And suddenly, more than anything she wanted *not* to see him.

She wanted to keep him safely in her head and heart as a dream father. Someone she could love without any of the reservations, angers and uncertainties that there were in her love for Mo. Someone she could *pretend* would love her too...

'Matty,' she said, stopping in the middle of the long, village street, 'I don't think I can!'

'Course you can,' he said. 'We ent come this far to turn back.'

Without looking to see if she was following him he walked on down a lane, signposted *Owlcombe*. Dragging her feet, Bella trailed behind him. The pictures which came crowding into her head were dire.

Oliver appalled. Oliver furious. Oliver marching herself and Matty down a bleak country road towards a grim building marked POLICE.

The lane twisted and turned. Between its high, leafless hedges the twilight which had lasted all afternoon, deepened towards darkness. Somewhere in a field a cow coughed harshly and from a distance they heard the hollow, tremulous cry of an owl.

Whistling a kind of up-hill, down-dale tune Matty trudged on till they came to a crossroads.

Owlcombe, said the sign, *2 miles*.

'But it said that in Stretton,' wailed Bella. 'And we must

93

have walked one mile already!'

'Na!' scoffed Matty. 'We been half a mile at most.'

As if the sign's unreliability were his fault, Bella stamped huffily away from him. Five minutes later the first snowflakes began to fall. At first they seemed to shape themselves slowly out of the murky air but it was not long before they were swarming around Bella and Matty like cold white bees, crowding along their eyelashes, stinging their faces.

A car growled past them, the beams of its headlights full of the furious snowdance, its windscreen wipers thrashing to and fro. In the narrow road, Matty felt its slipstream brush his sleeve.

'They come close!' he exclaimed. ' I reckons they didn't see us!'

He stood still. Water dripped off his nose and ears. If the blizzard made it difficult for drivers to see them, walking in the narrow lane was dangerous. A little way ahead he could see a patch of black against the whitening spread of the hillside.

'There's woods up here,' he said, tugging at Bella's coat. 'We can shelter under the trees for a bit.'

When they reached the wood, however, they found it offered more than shelter. For beside the stile which led into it a finger post leaned and pointed. *Footpath*, it announced. *To Owlcombe*.

Chapter 23

'D'you suppose it's a short cut?' asked Bella hopefully.

Matty was dubious. His last foster father, Gary, had been a great one for short cuts. He had hiked Matty all over the countryside, hoping perhaps to wear him out or distract him from going on safari by himself. And although Matty was much better at map reading than he was, Gary had hogged the map to himself. Most of *his* short cuts turned out to be long voyages into the unknown...

It was less bitter in the wood than on the wind-raked lane and at first, the canopy of branches above them saved them from the worst of the snowfall. But in the dusk the path was hard to see and in places where the trees thinned out the snow already lay like a white crust over everything. Only here and there clumps of rusty brown bracken broke through it.

'We're lost,' cried Bella as they stumbled into a clearing where she was sure they had been before.

Baffled by the dizzy whirligig of flakes, Matty cut back under the trees. Here, except for the glimmer given off by the snow, it was totally dark.

Bella slumped against a tree trunk and slithered into a sitting position. Her hands and feet were numb and hurting at the same time.

'I can't go another step,' she shouted after him.

Turning back he came and squatted in front of her.

'You has to,' he said.

That too was something he believed. No matter how bad things got you had to grit your teeth and keep going. Sooner or later the snow would stop, the path would end, daylight would dawn.

'We were crazy to come,' she said, on the verge of tears. 'Even if we get out of this wood we won't find Oliver. And even if we do find Oliver, he won't want to know.'

A heap of soft snow slid from a branch and splattered on to Matty's bare head.

'Bog off!' he grumbled.

Then slipping off his rucksack, he retrieved the crumpled wig, pulled it down over his ears like a hat and gave Bella a wide grin. The eerie snowlight made his skin look faintly green, his smile sinister.

What am I doing here, thought Bella, *with this… this Changeling…*

Moaning softly she began to bump herself rhythmically against the tree.

'Mo!' she wailed. 'I want Mo!'

She closed her eyes and her rocking grew wilder, her cries louder. Matty who was used to seeing people in this kind of distress, called up all his courage and slapped her face hard. His icy fingers burned her skin and she gasped to a stop. Tears brimmed in her eyes but did not fall.

'Listen, Greensleeves,' he said. 'That's why we're here, ent it? To find your Mam? But first we got to get to your Dad…'

'Leave me alone,' she murmured. 'I'm too cold. Too tired.'

'I ent leavin' you,' he said.

He would not believe that the story which began for him when Bella came flying to his rescue, was going to end here, like this. So far he had trusted in the signs. And he had *made* things go the way he wanted. He was not going to give up now. Sliding his hand into his rucksack he touched the snow globe for luck. Snow, after all, was part of this story. Beneath the globe he felt the package which held the remains of their lunch. Tweaking out a sandwich he held it out towards her.

'You'll feel better,' he said, 'with a bite of somethin' inside you!'

With the back of her hand she mopped her eyes and

then shuffled further down into the heap of dry, dead leaves at the foot of the tree.

'I'm not hungry,' she said. 'I want to sleep. I'll be all right if I have a little sleep. Warm under the leaves – like the Babes in the Wood.'

Vaguely Matty remembered his Gran telling him that story. He shook his head and gently but firmly pressed the sandwich against Bella's lips.

'Those kids wouldn't of just gone to sleep,' he said. 'They'd of died. That's what happens when you gets too cold and lets yourself drift off.'

Bella grimaced but nibbled at the edge of the bread. He persisted, would not let her stop until the sandwich was finished. Then he gave her an apple. Its skin was leathery, its flesh spongy and it tasted of nothing. But she ate it.

Standing up, Matty reached for her hands and hauled her to her feet. She neither helped nor hindered but he was sturdier and stronger than he looked. When she was upright the numbness in her feet, made her stagger against him so he put his arm round her and together they tottered out of the trees. Bella felt like someone hobbling to the end of a three-legged race but she was glad of his support and of his warmth against her side.

Out in the clearing again they found the snow had stopped. Through a ragged tear in the clouds the moon shone down, turning everything to silver. And now, between the snowy ridges of bracken, they could see once more the clear line of the path.

Chapter 24

When they emerged from the wood they saw, only a short distance away, the comforting twinkle of the village street lights. Walking in the snow furrows made by cars they passed the entrance to a farm and then a pair of cottages. The shadows of hedgerow trees lay across the lane like black iron bars.

Bella slowed to a stop. 'The place we're looking for might be *any*where,' she groaned.

Without speaking Matty drew away from her and pointed. Immediately on their left was a gatepost and clear and sharp in the moonlight the name was carved into the stone. *Guinevere's Bower.* Between the posts a five barred gate stood open and beyond it a pebbled driveway wound towards the dark bulk of a building.

So Oliver's house, at least, was real.

They turned into the drive. Bella's fuddled brain tried to shape phrases to introduce and explain themselves to Oliver. But her heart was beating so hard it took away her breath and she doubted she would be able to speak at all.

The house, when they reached it, was not a bit like her imagined medieval tower. It was a square, stone house facing out over its own lawns to the village. Like a child's drawing it had a chimney in the middle of its roof, three windows upstairs and two downstairs, flanking the front door. The downstairs windows shone with a soft, flickering light as if the rooms behind them were lit by candles.

To the right of the house the spreading branches of a cedar tree, luminous with snow, sheltered four cars, drawn up higgledy-piggledy, on the gravel.

'He's having a party!' exclaimed Bella, for they could

see the front door stood ajar and through it floated the sounds of laughter and music. 'I can't tell him who I am in *public*!' she said.

Matty saw the problem. He tried the door of the nearest car.

'If one of 'em's open,' he said, 'we can climb inside and wait.'

Out in the lane they heard a vehicle approaching over the hardening ruts of snow.

'I reckons it's comin' here,' said Matty.

Bent double he scuttled from car to car, trying all the doors. The third one yielded and he beckoned to Bella. The moon slipped behind a frayed edge of cloud and a few snowflakes idled down. The gears of the approaching car changed once, twice, and then they heard the crunch of its tyres as it turned on to the gravel.

Grazing hands and knees, Bella and Matty scrambled into the back of the Renault and pulled the door to. The car smelled of cigarette smoke and stale perfume. They ducked down, squeezing themselves into the cramped space between the front and back seats.

The lights of the new arrival swept across the roof. There was a long pause followed by the bang of a car door and the rumble of men's voices. Footsteps squeaked on the snow. Then there was silence.

After a few minutes Bella climbed on to the seat. She could see now that the house door was closed. Across the lighted windows the silhouettes of people drifted to and fro like ghosts.

'Now what are we going to do?' she said.

There was a tartan rug in the back of the car and a tweed jacket hanging from the driver's headrest. Matty tucked the rug around Bella and, still lying on the floor, he huddled himself into the jacket.

To take their minds off the pain of the cold he told all the jokes and riddles he could remember. Bella tried to listen and respond but gradually his voice faded out of her hearing as she began to put together a picture.

It was a picture of Oliver's party. Warm firelight winked on jewels and glinted on teeth as people circled and smiled. And there, at the centre, was Mo. Mo in her slinky black party frock, her Indian silk scarf draped gracefully across her shoulders. Blue eyes smouldering, hair shining like polished mahogany, she raised her hand for Oliver to fill her glass and her silver bangles tinkled together like bells.

Oliver smiled down at her, his lopsided smile dimpling his face.

'Welcome home,' he whispered.

Mo lowered her eyes, sipped her wine.

'Oliver,' she said. 'Remember we have a…'

'Hush,' he said.

'But Monty,' she persisted. 'I must tell you about…'

He stepped back, his face in shadow.

'So cold,' murmured Mo. 'I'm so cold!'

She leaned over to rest her head against his shoulder and the picture slipped out of focus as Bella felt herself sliding… falling… floating away…

Chapter 25

Bella woke when Matty, trying to lever himself out of the well of the car, dug his fingers into her arm.

'Ouch!' she grumbled.

'I got to get out,' he said. 'I needs a pee.'

His teeth were clacking together and all the use had gone out of his hands so that Bella had to sit up and open the door for him.

He seemed to be gone for ages. When he came back he told her that the house door was wide open. Bella looked at him stupidly, wondering whether he meant they should just walk straight in.

'People are startin' to leave the party,' he explained. 'So you has to come out o' there. Quick!'

Moaning with the effort she tumbled herself into the snow. No more seemed to have fallen and the sky was now clear, the moon sailing high among the stars. Everything glistened with frost. She felt entirely stiff, as if her flesh had frozen to her bones.

Matty crept round the back of the cars, keeping in the shadow of the tree. Bella followed him. When she glanced to her left she could see the brightly lit doorway and someone standing on the step. Behind her the village was in darkness, the lights all out. It must be very late.

'Here,' hissed Matty. 'There's a path…'

It was pitch dark round this side of the house but the untrodden snow gave just enough light for them to see where a paved path led towards a gate in a hedge. Beyond the hedge was a small enclosed garden and then another gate.

'It's the back yard,' said Matty, peering through the wrought iron bars.

His cold fingers fumbled with the latch and the gate creaked open. The cobbled yard lay in the angle between the main part of the house and a lean-to kitchen. It was protected to the north by a high wall and on the fourth side there was a stone building with a stout wooden door. Matty tried this but it was locked.

For a moment they stood shivering outside the small circles of light cast by the kitchen window. Then Matty sneaked forward and standing on tiptoe, peeped inside.

There was no-one there. In the middle of the room stood a pine table heaped with dirty plates and dishes half full of food. Cold as he was, Matty's mouth watered. He felt, as his Gran would say, as empty as a poor man's pocket. He whispered to Bella to come and see but she would not move.

Looking at her Matty knew they must not stay out in the cold much longer. Stealthily he lifted the latch on the back door. But the door was bolted on the inside. From round the front of the house they could hear sounds of merriment and a car engine revving up. The light in the kitchen seemed to flicker and leaving the door he moved to the window again.

A man had come into the room. He was standing at the table but facing the other way so that all Matty could see of him was his blue sweater and jeans and the mop of black curls that brushed his collar. He seemed to be filling a carton with party left-overs.

Oliver. It must be Oliver.

Suddenly scared by the enormity of what they were about to do, Matty hesitated for a long moment before raising his hand and tapping sharply on the glass.

Chapter 26

As soon as the door opened Bella knew she had found her father. Although his hair was long and he was thinner and paler than he looked on the television screen, he had the same golden brown eyes, the same slightly crooked

102

mouth which made him look amused and exasperated at the same time.

'What the blazes!' he exclaimed, staring down at them both.

His first thought was that they must be the children of some of his guests. Brought here and left to sleep in the car while their parents enjoyed the party. Though surely none of his friends had children who looked like this!

Matty waited for Bella to speak but after her first quick glance at Oliver she was utterly silent, gazing down at her feet. And even though he was not quite touching her Matty could feel her trembling.

'If you lets us in,' he said to Oliver, 'she'll be able to tell you everythin'.'

'I think you must have made some mistake,' said Oliver.

'Please,' said Matty, remembering how it often helped to be polite.

Dazed, Oliver stepped back and taking this as a signal Matty pushed Bella into the kitchen.

'Hang on!' said Oliver. 'I didn't say...'

But it was too late. The two children stood between him and the table, snow from their shoes melting into puddles on his tiled floor. Were they New Age travellers? Runaways? Children involved in a car accident in the snowy lanes?

From his sitting room the murmur of voices reminded him of the ordinary, everyday world he had left only minutes ago. Any moment now someone would come into the kitchen to see what he was doing. Quickly shutting the door to the yard, he said, 'Wait here. And don't dare move!' Then picking up the box of goodies he had been packing he strode across the kitchen and went

103

back to his guests.

Matty looked hungrily at the assorted food on the table.

'Don't touch it,' pleaded Bella. Long painful shivers ran through her, part fear, part cold. 'What d'you suppose he's doing?' she asked.

'Gettin' rid of his party people,' said Matty. 'He ent goin' to tell 'em *we're* here, that's for sure!' Steering Bella to the nearest chair he drew off her gloves and began to chafe her hands. But his own were so cold it was like rubbing two stones together.

Oliver seemed to be gone for ages. The noise of talk and laughter from the far side of the door made Matty wonder if the party had begun all over again.

'D'you think he hopes we'll just give up and go away?' whispered Bella.

'Huh!' said Matty, pinching a sausage roll. 'He don't know me!'

The sausage was still warm, the pastry so flaky it clung to his frozen lips. He took another and offered it to Bella but she scowled and turned her head away. Now that she was actually inside Oliver's house Bella felt as though she had broken through the invisible barrier which kept the imaginary world safely separate from the real one. In the real world her father was going to be more than she could deal with.

In sudden panic she leapt to her feet. But it was too late. Even as Matty reached out to restrain her they heard the front door slam. There was the sound of cars turning, pulling away on the gravel and seconds later, in the silence that washed back through the house, Oliver returned to the kitchen.

Chapter 27

He did not advance into the room but stood in the doorway, looking at them. Seeing off his guests had given him no time to think and besides, not having to drive that night, he had drunk more than usual and now felt as if he had fur growing on the inside of his head.

'So you're still here,' he said.

He noted the flakes of pastry on Matty's chin and Bella's start of fear — or guilt. What if they were some kind of decoy being used by villains who intended to rob him? In the last year *Guinevere's Bower* had been burgled twice.

'Right,' he said, running his hands through his hair till it stood out from his head in stiff black corkscrews. 'I'm going to ring the police.'

'No!' cried Bella.

Matty stepped quickly to her side. 'Ent you goin' to ask us what we wants, first?' he said.

'Hell's teeth!' muttered Oliver.

He saw that Matty's request was reasonable but he did not want to be reasonable. He wanted to get to bed. Moreover their arrival on his doorstep at such an hour was positively *not* reasonable. Maybe at three o'clock in the afternoon it would have been different. The stuff of an amusing story he could later tell his friends…

While he remained silent Matty was watching him closely, aware of his uncertainty and of his slight tipsiness.

'I'll give you five minutes,' said Oliver at last. 'Any longer and I'll be unconscious.'

Bella peeped at him under her lashes. On those last words his voice had changed and he sounded quizzical, warm, wry, the way he sounded on the Golden Sunbursts commercial. She knew this sense of his familiarity was false but nevertheless her courage returned and taking a deep breath she started to speak.

Everything she wanted to say came out broken and muddled and not at all the way she had planned it earlier. And it took much longer than five minutes. Bella told how her mother had gone missing and how she was afraid of being sent into care. She explained how she had nobody she could confide in except Matty, who was already in care, and was running away…

'Matty?' asked Oliver.

'Me,' said Matty.

'His real name's Matthew,' explained Bella.

'Matthew! I thought he was your *sister*!'

Matty snatched off the wig and threw it in the corner. Confronted with his scarred, naked head, Oliver buried his face in his hands.

'What on earth,' he asked, 'has this… this rigmarole got to do with *me*?'

At his irritated tone Bella crumpled. 'It's not a rigmarole!' she cried. 'It's the truth. We came to you because we found your address in the newspaper. And because you… I mean because years ago Mo was your… that is, when you were young you and Mo were…'

The thing Bella had to say would not be spoken. It was too difficult. But what she could not say, Matty could.

'She's tryin' to tell you,' he said, 'that you're the properest bloke to help her, see. Because you're her *Dad*.'

Many times Bella had tried to envisage this scene. She had imagined Oliver horrified, scornful, suspicious, furious. Occasionally she had dared to imagine him pleased. But never in all the stories she had told herself, had she expected him to do what he did next.

He threw his head back, his mouth fell open – and he laughed.

Chapter 28

'I don't believe this is happening to me,' murmured Oliver. 'It's too bizarre.'

He had stopped laughing and his face had a grim, weary look. He felt as if time had given a great lurch, thrusting him back to the days when orphans commonly wandered the winter roads and died forgotten in some flooded ditch.

'I suppose you're hungry too?' he said.

Matty nodded and curtly telling them to help themselves to some food, Oliver disappeared again through the inner door.

'Is he going to let us stay, d'you think?' asked Bella whose eyes burned and blurred with sleep.

Matty did not answer. He was afraid that Oliver had sneaked off to 'phone the police and, just in case, he hurriedly devoured scraps of Coronation chicken, slivers of salmon and half a cold baked potato. Bella watched him for a moment and then picked listlessly at a slice of quiche.

Oliver seemed gone a long while and by the time he returned Bella's head was drooping and Matty had fallen asleep with his face in a plate of crisps.

'He ought to be put to bed,' said Bella, coming to with a start.

She could see the faint violet veins in the naked whiteness of Matty's neck and for some reason it made her want to cry.

'He's so brave,' she murmured, looking up at Oliver. 'He puts up with so much. He saved my life tonight. If it weren't for him I'd be dead in the forest.'

She was a plain little thing, he thought. Apart from her slanting, sea-green eyes. He wanted to laugh again at the thought of Owlcombe Brake being considered as a forest but he could see the pain in her face and he already felt ashamed of his earlier laughter.

'Listen,' he said. 'I've put sleeping bags for you and the boy in the spare room and in my study.'

She blinked in surprise and started to thank him but he brushed it aside with a frown. 'In the morning,' he said, 'I hand you over to the proper authorities. I'm not doing it now only because I'm just too shot to deal with it. Make no mistake. I am *not* about to become your fairy god-father.'

'No,' said Bella, glowering down at the table. 'But I don't believe you're not my *actual* father. Mo told me you were. And Mo *never* lies to me.'

Oliver groaned. Not for the first time it seemed to him that whenever he tried to do a good deed it turned on him – like some sharp-fanged animal he was attempting to release from a trap.

'Whatever you choose to believe,' he said, between gritted teeth, 'I am not your father. Positively and absolutely I am not!'

'How d'you know?' she demanded stubbornly. 'It sometimes happens by accident…'

Was that why Oliver had deserted Mo? she wondered. Perhaps he had not known about the baby. Perhaps Mo had not told him because, being so young, she was very frightened and tried not to believe it herself.

Seeing him face to face Bella desperately wanted

Oliver to be the sort of man she had imagined him to be; strong, kind, honourable, *good*. Not the rat of Mo's story.

But Oliver was shaking his head, his expression exasperated.

'No. No. No!' he said. 'It's not possible.' He did not feel up to this discussion and spoke more brutally than he intended. 'I have *never* had a child,' he went on, 'either by accident or design. I'm not... I'm not a lady's man. And I can't imagine why your mother told you what she did.'

The coldness of his voice and the implied criticism of Mo, stung Bella into the tears she had been holding back for hours. Unstopped they trickled down her nose and dripped on to the table.

'I want Mo,' she sobbed. 'I need her so... And I know she'd not have gone off and left me like this... without a word...'

Still weeping she rummaged in her bag, finding the old photograph of her mother and pushing it across the table towards Oliver.

'That's her,' she cried. 'What if she's been... what if she's in... what if something *awful's* happened to her?'

Oliver glanced at the grey, crumpled picture of Mo and once more shook his head. Bella's grief and fear seemed sincere. But apart from the fact he had grown up in Orbury, the story she told bore no relation to himself or his past.

As the grandfather clock in his sitting room began to strike four, Matty stirred, smacking his lips together and rolling his forehead in the crisps.

'Please,' whispered Bella. 'You have to help me! You must! Without Matty I'd never have come to you but he believes I was *meant* to come. He thinks finding your address when I needed you was a *sign*. If you hand us over

109

to the police he'll be so let down! He'll lose his faith in himself…'

Worn out with everything that had happened in the last week, she could not explain why she felt that Matty's faith in himself was so important. In any case there was no point. Oliver's eyes were closed and he looked bored.

'Why are grown-ups so mean to children?' she said, swallowing her tears and standing up. 'If we were older you wouldn't just dump us on somebody else! You'd listen properly to what we had to say…'

'At four o'clock in the morning,' said Oliver, 'I doubt I'd listen to God himself!'

Bella placed her hand on Matty's shoulder and shook him awake. Tumbling off his chair he stood between them, swaying blearily, and over his head she glared at Oliver.

'Ever since Mo told me about you,' she said, 'I've so much wanted you to be my father. But now I've met you I'm really, really glad that after all, you're *not*!'

SATURDAY

Oliver did not wake until nine. His head was thumping and his mouth tasted foul. With a grouchy sense that something else was wrong he sat up. Then he remembered.

He had planned a quiet weekend: reading; music; a little work; a long walk; a lunch, perhaps, with friends or with his mother in Waterham. Now all that was turned upside down. Pulling on a pair of jeans he staggered downstairs.

'I'll give them breakfast,' he said to himself. 'And then I'll hand them over…'

When he saw the state of the kitchen he was appalled. Oliver was fastidious. He hated mess and disorder. So, clattering the dirty plates together, he began to clear up. He was too ill-tempered to notice that most of the left-over food was missing and it was not until he swept up a packet of Golden Sunbursts that he paused. Frowning he stared at it. *That* had not been put out with the party food! Beside it, he noticed now, were two empty bowls and picking them up he found, tucked beneath one of them, a folded square of paper.

Slowly, his heart misgiving him, he opened it.

Dear Mr Montfort, he read. *Thank you for letting us sleep here last night. I'm sorry we've taken some of your food but as you can't help us we can't stay and we may really need it. Yours sincerely, Bella Partridge and Matthew Byrd.*

Oliver read it twice. Behind the neatly written words he heard Bella's voice, husky with weariness and disappointment. Slumping on to the nearest chair he gazed out of the window at white fields criss-crossed with dark hedges and trees like dense black scribbles against a pearly sky. A cold, unfriendly landscape. And somewhere, two scared children, throwing themselves on its mercy as they fled from him.

He looked once more at the note. If they had been dishonest and the story they told him a tissue of lies, Bella would surely not have written – much less signed – it. Bella Partridge. Something stirred at the back of Oliver's mind but he could not bring it into focus.

I should have foreseen this, he thought. *That they would run away again.*

Prompted by an uneasy mixture of feelings, he slipped the note into his pocket and went to fetch his coat. It was unlikely that the children had gone far yet. Probably they would make for Stretton. If he took the car he would soon catch up with them.

Matty had woken Bella before dawn. He planned on catching the bus back to Waterham. Once there they could decide what to do next. Meanwhile it was important to leave as quickly as possible. So, while most of Owlcombe still slept, he led Bella through the village and out among the deserted fields.

Slithering and stumbling on the slippery surface of the road, she lagged behind him. Since she had scrambled grumpily out of her sleeping bag in Oliver's spare room she had hardly spoken. Her head was pounding and her throat felt as though it were stuck full of thorns.

'I reckons you ent very well,' said Matty, stopping for the third time to wait for her.

She tried to smile at him but he wasn't deceived. She was so white that the peppering of last summer's freckles across her nose and cheekbones lay like a dark shadow on her face.

116

Above them the lightening sky was the colour of cement, a flat, heavy grey that seemed to be resting its weight on the treetops. If it started to snow again he knew they would be in real trouble.

'What we needs,' he said, 'is a place you can rest up a bit. A barn or some such…'

What I need, thought Bella miserably, *is home. And Mo…*

Leaving her for a moment, Matty climbed the bank. Through the thorny network of the hedge he could see the fields rising towards the crest of a hill, and about half a mile away, in the lee of a small wood, a long, low farmhouse. The lights in its downstairs windows winked cheerily at him through the gloom.

'Yeah! Go for it!' he muttered, using one of Dave's favourite expressions of encouragement.

For where there was a farm there were bound to be barns and shippens and other outbuildings.

Returning to Bella he took her hand and gently, as if she were his Gran, he led her a hundred yards further along the lane to where a five-barred-gate in the hedge opened into the fields.

Chapter 30

By the time Oliver arrived back at *Guinevere's Bower* the morning was more than half over. He had driven round the lanes for an hour without seeing any sign of Bella and Matty. It was as if they had been spirited away by magic. If only he had rung the police the moment they had walked into his kitchen he would be free of the whole business by now.

Tugging at his ear lobe he went slowly into his sitting

117

room and hovered over the telephone. But while he was still rehearsing the words he would speak, it rang.

'Oliver?' said his mother. 'Where've you been? I've been trying to reach you for ages! I was hoping you'd come for lunch today.'

'Sorry, Ma,' he said. 'I don't think I can.'

He began to explain why and found himself telling her the whole story. It took a long time and for most of it she listened in silence. Once or twice, surprisingly, she laughed.

'Hm,' she murmured when he trailed to a stop. 'It might be good for you...'

'What?'

'To have your tidy life made untidy for once... not to have everything under control.'

Oliver scowled. What his mother did not guess was that it was only by exercising such control that he kept his old childhood bogeys of fear and boredom at bay.

'The question is, Ma,' he said sharply, 'what do I do now?'

In her quiet, incisive way she said, 'Well, Son. You must report the whole thing, of course. But since you've already left it so long perhaps you should take another few minutes and try to check the *facts* the children gave you. Did you get their names?'

He told her and there was a short pause. Then she giggled.

'A Byrd in the hand,' she said. 'And a Partridge in a pear tree!'

He could just see her, sitting by the window in her upstairs lounge, gazing out over the delicate spires and colonnaded crescents of Waterham, her jewelled fingers tapping the arm of her chair, smiling at her own joke.

'Ma!' he protested.

But she had lightened his mood and when he finished speaking to her he went on for another hour, telephoning various people. First he tried directory enquiries where he confirmed Bella's address in Orbury but found the 'phone was disconnected. Then he rang a friend who lived not far from Pavilion Street and she agreed to go down and check whether there was anyone at Number 21.

'No-one,' she said when she rang back. 'Though I knocked hard enough to waken the dead. Tried next door too but whoever lives there was out. What *is* all this about, Monty?'

'Tell you later,' he said. And went on to contact John Hemmings who worked in the administrative centre for the county police.

'No adults reported missing last week,' said Hemmings. 'No bodies found. I'm pretty sure of that. A couple of teenagers have gone walkabout. A mazed old man was discovered wandering along the railway line at Torsham. And there's a ten-year-old lad – a boy in care – who's taken off for the umpteenth time...'

'Ah!' said Oliver. And he asked for the boy's name.

'Don't believe I heard it. Oh yes... come to think of it... it was Robin... Sparrow... some kind of...'

'Byrd?'

'Yeah. Right. Some kind of bird!'

Exhilarated by this small success, Oliver was also pleased to find that the children had not lied to him. But returning to his kitchen he was cast down again by the clutter of stale food, the puddled floor, the still unwashed dishes. Unable to think clearly in the chaos, he turned on the taps and watched the water cascade over the dirty plates. Steam rose, hazing the window and blurring his view of the snowy fields.

'All the same,' he muttered. 'I can't go on – fooling around like this! The only possible thing to do is report them to the Orbury police.'

Chapter 31

The barn Matty found was large and dim and draughty. Several fields away from the farmhouse, it stood in the angle between two high hedges. Outside, sheep huddled against its walls or browsed the thin, frosted grass. Inside, bales of hay bound with twine were stacked almost to the rafters, except for the end nearest the door where trusses of it were strewn loosely about the earthen floor.

Here and there snow rimmed the underside of the sagging roof tiles and in the corners cobwebs hung in great dusty swags. But it was mostly dry and the thick stone walls kept out the wind which they could hear whining softly at a chink between the doorpost and the door.

Snuggled into the hay which Matty piled around her Bella drifted into a deep, dreamless sleep as though the sweet, summer scent of it had drugged her. While she slept, Matty wrestled with some of the bales, building a sort of hay igloo to hide her from any intruder coming into the barn.

When he was satisfied with this shelter he went to sit where a beam of light came slanting between the rafters. Opening his rucksack he saw his snow globe lying like an egg in a nest of the food he had taken from *Guinevere's Bower*. He lifted it out, wiped it clean with his sleeve, and then peered into it as he nibbled a couple of soggy crackers.

Inside the globe the light coming in from the roof dwindled away to nothing. He could only just see the tree and the girl but all colour was drained out of them. Her holly green coat looked black, her fiery hair as grey as ashes. Without much hope Matty shook it but the snowflakes rose sluggishly and settled without sparkle. Clearly today it had nothing to tell him.

With a shrug he replaced the globe in his bag. Sometimes, he knew, his signs misled him. Or turned out not to be signs at all. But, because of how and when it happened, he had been very sure that the finding of Oliver's address had been a *true* sign.

Thinking about Oliver, Matty decided he had been kinder than he needed to be, considering he was *not* Bella's father. *I reckons he's like most people*, he thought. *Wants to do the right thing — but don't want to take on anything that could mean trouble…*

Restless now with pent up energy he returned to Bella. She lay on her back with her mouth slightly open, snoring faintly.

'Your throat'll be dry as old sandpaper, Greensleeves,' he said.

Because it was he who had persuaded her to set out on this quest for her father he felt badly about the way it was turning out. Propping his bag up beside her he took out a carton of orange juice he had found in Oliver's fridge and set it down where she would be bound to see it if she woke. Then, after poking around the barn for a time and finding nothing of interest, he went to the door and stood listening.

He could hear no human sound. Only the frail bleating

121

of new-born lambs from the surrounding fields and the occasional 'Wark Wark' of a carrion crow. Wincing at the squealing of its iron hinges, he tugged open the barn door and slipped outside.

Chapter 32

Bella slept all morning. When she woke she was confused by the darkness and mystified by the prickling of the hay against her chin. Her throat was burning and her head felt as if it were gripped in a tight steel band. Remembering at last where she was, she crawled out of her shelter and saw Matty was not in the barn.

Snarlygogs to him, she thought.

Retreating into the hiding place she tore open the carton of orange juice and drank in huge, noisy gulps.

'Whoa Gosling!' cautioned Mo's voice in her head. 'All that cold juice on an empty stomach! And don't be greedy – what about your brother?'

It was ages since Bella had heard Mo speak to her like that and now her aching head seemed to be playing tricks on her.

'Stupid!' she snarled. 'You mean "What about the *'other'*…"'

There was no answer from Mo and overwhelmed with misery Bella cried, 'I *hate* you, Mo! Why have you deserted me? And why did you tell me Oliver was my father?'

Setting the carton down she wiped her lips with the back of her hand. 'I hate him too,' she said. But as soon as she started to think about Oliver she realised her disappointment in him was unjust. The fault lay not in him but in Mo's words and in the foolish daydreams she herself had built on them...

She was still brooding over this when a harsh, grating sound from somewhere very close by, made her jump. Holding her breath she sat without moving as the light in her shelter brightened and the grating noise changed to a squeal. Someone had come into the barn! There was a muffled bang and a click and she heard footsteps shuffling towards her. She was trying to bury herself in the hay, when Matty stooped in under the bales.

'Hey Greensleeves!' he cried. 'It's proper country out there!'

Smelling of cold and grinning widely, he seemed unaware he had frightened her.

'Where've you been?' she snapped, her fear turning to anger. 'You shouldn't go outside! What if someone saw you?'

'Like George and Arnie, you means,' he joked. His eyes shone. Cold and exercise had made him feel better and arching backwards until he was bent in a hoop, he edged crabwise towards her.

'I'm a MONSTER,' he growled. 'And I'm comin' to GET you!'

'I'm not afraid of monsters,' said Bella, pushing him over.

Matty rolled himself up like a hedgehog and lay still.

'What sort of things would they... would George and Arnie do to you if they did catch you?' she asked.

'You knows. I told you.'

But he had not told her everything and did not intend to. He had not mentioned how they put itching powder in his bed; how they nicked him with the point of their penknives; how they singed his hair, when he had any;

how they pressed their cigarette ends against his bare flesh, when they could catch him and hold him still.

Guessing by his silence that there were things he was holding back, she said, 'You should tell your guardians at Elmbridge House.'

Matty snickered. He tried to explain that his 'guardians,' as she called them, were mostly well meaning but were too busy, changed over too often, had short fuses or were generally cack-handed in dealing with kids. Much of what happened they pretended not to see, not wanting more trouble than they already had. And lots of the kids were big trouble!

'I don't allus behave, either,' he confessed. 'And bein' as I do runners all the time they has to give me punishments. As an example, see.'

'What sort of punishments?'

Matty uncurled and sat up. 'Things like cleanin' the bogs. Or sortin' rubbish from the kitchen. And once they made me spend a whole day pickin' up stones in the garden. I picked so many I built a whole hill of 'em. Byrd's Hill they calls it. Pretty name ent it?'

Bella thought Matty was very cool. In his place she would have stamped and screamed and fought with all her might. Or perhaps instead she would have taken flight deep inside herself. Refused to speak. Become like the living dead.

Matty, however, felt only contempt for those who ill-treated him. And one way to show that contempt was never to admit he was hurt.

'I doesn't fret over it,' he said. 'I reckons I were born cheerful!'

'I reckon you were,' said Bella.

Ashamed of her own sharpness with him earlier, she

124

offered him the last of the juice. He tipped the carton to his lips and in one swallow drank what was left.

'Good thing I went explorin',' he observed. ''Cos we ent got any more juice but I found a tap. It's down in the farm-yard. There's people about now but when it's dark I'll fetch some water.'

For the first time the impossibility of their situation dawned on Bella.

'How long d'you think we're *staying* here?' she moaned.

She was suddenly feeling awful again. Too ill even to talk about it. As Matty undid another packet of Oliver's food and tried to persuade her to eat, she felt herself slide away from him, sinking like a stone into sleep.

Chapter 33

While Oliver was setting his kitchen to rights he came across Matty's wig, lying like a squashed black cat in the corner where the boy had tossed it. As he picked it up a clear, sharp image of the children flashed across his inward eye and he groaned.

'Stop this!' he told himself. 'They'll be fine. I always was. And the boy's far more streetwise than I could ever have been.'

Putting together a quick snack of left-overs he drifted into his sitting room. Rather than ring the police in Orbury he decided that after he had eaten he would drive down to the police station in Stretton. Sergeant Hassell there was an old friend and it would be easier to explain everything to him than to strangers.

He had hardly finished his belated breakfast, however,

before his sleepless night caught up with him and it was a full hour before he was startled awake again by the shrilling of the telephone.

'Thought I'd just ring to see if you'd resolved your problem yet,' said his mother.

How well she knows my tendency to dither, thought Oliver. *And to put things off!* Cradling the receiver between chin and shoulder, he rubbed his eyes and yawned.

'If you hadn't 'phoned this very moment,' he fibbed. 'I'd now be on my way to see Brian Hassell.'

'Have you checked the children's story?'

'Don't nag me, Ma. Yes. And basically they seem to have told the truth...'

'Ah!' she said. 'So they do come from Orbury!'

There was something in her voice which made him think she had more to say and tweaking crossly at his ear, Oliver waited.

'You remember those drama classes you went to in Orbury?' she said. 'When you were in the sixth form? Aren't I right in thinking there was a little auburn-haired girl in that group – funny and bright and slightly flighty? Her name, I think, was Maureen... Moira...something like that...'

'No,' said Oliver. 'It wasn't Maureen. It was Morag.'

As soon as he spoke the name the memory which had flickered at the back of his mind when he had read Bella's note took shape. He could see the bare, shabby room where the drama classes were held. And sun shining on a girl's long red hair as she danced on a table, feet tapping out the rhythm of the song she was singing.

'Bella calls her Mo,' he said to his mother. 'I suppose it *could* be her. But I hardly knew the girl. Why the devil would she have told Bella I was her father?'

126

'I've no idea, Son. Except…'

'Except what?'

'In that same drama group there was another boy called Oliver. Daventry his name was. Oliver Daventry. His mother, you know, worked at Frazer's in the…'

'Ma!' exclaimed Oliver. 'For someone so aged your memory is phenomenal! You're quite right. We always called him Dav. I remember he was as smooth and dapper as a fifties film star. But not much of an actor!'

'Actor or no,' said his mother smugly. 'He went on to drama school in London. So you see it could be a case of mistaken identity. The mother not saying enough, the girl putting two and two together to make five.'

Wondering if his mother had hit on the truth Oliver frowned. He did not relish the idea of being mistaken for Oliver Daventry.

'I must go, Ma,' he said. 'I've wasted far too much time already. But thanks for ringing. At least I know now that both children were who they said they were.'

'Are,' she corrected him. 'Let's hope they still *are*…'

Replacing the receiver, Oliver was shaken by a sudden fear. He did not want to be involved in Bella and Matty's story but like it or not, he was. Moreover, both as a teacher and as a man, he felt strongly that all adults had a duty of care towards all children. What if, because of his hopeless shilly-shallying, these two had come to some further harm?

Snatching his keys from the hook in the kitchen he pulled on his coat and ran out to his car.

127

Chapter 34

For the rest of the day Bella slept and woke, slept and woke, while Matty prowled around the barn, played among the hay bales, studied the map again. He supposed they ought to go back to Orbury once Bella was well enough. But for all sorts of reasons that idea had no appeal.

As the hours crept on to mid-afternoon it grew very dark inside the building. Small creatures rustled in the hay and something larger gnawed on wood among the rafters. Inside her igloo Bella tossed and turned and muttered. Matty crawled in to look at her and she leapt up, flinging wisps of grass in all directions.

'I'm so *dry!*' she wailed.

'There ent any juice left, remember,' said Matty.

She stared at him as though she had never seen him before. 'Hasn't Mo come home from work yet?' she said.

Alarmed, Matty picked up the empty juice carton and telling her he would not be long he went outside.

Here, where the lying snow cast its own cold, shadowless light, it was murky but not yet dark. Keeping close to the hedge he climbed to the brow of the hill and looked down on the farm. Through a gap in its outbuildings he could see light fanning out from the open door of the house, illuminating a battered jeep parked on the cobbles of the yard. The thrum thrum of its idling engine floated up to him.

As he started down the hill a light flurry of snow speckled his bare head, the straggling flakes scarcely seeming to reach the earth at all.

Like in me snow ball, he thought. *As though it's holdin' off. Waitin' for somethin' to happen.*

By the time he reached the first outbuilding he could hear tinny radio music above the sound of the jeep's engine. Sidling along the wall he made for the tap which was on the corner, just out of sight of the yard.

An elderly man, trousers tucked into muddy Wellington boots, was stooping over the rear of the jeep. From inside the vehicle a dog barked twice and the man told it to shut up. Taking advantage of the noise, Matty reached the tap and turned it on. Water gushed out filling his carton and overflowing it in seconds. It drenched his frozen hands and splashed over his trainers. When he tried to turn the tap off it stiffened and stuck tight with the water still pouring out, forming streams among the cobbles.

Setting the carton down Matty wrenched at the tap with both hands. To no avail. He heard the radio music stop and a woman's voice, artificially jolly, announce that it was four o'clock and time for the local news bulletin. His feet and the legs of Bella's dungarees were soaking wet and the streams of water were joining up, snaking towards the yard. Giving up the struggle, Matty grabbed the soggy carton and backed away into the shadows.

As he did so he heard the farmer open the door of the jeep so that the newsreader's voice blared out, the words carrying clearly across the stillness of the yard... 'A young woman,' said the newsreader, 'small and slender... with cropped chestnut hair and blue eyes...'

Matty knew he should escape while the dog was silent, the man out of sight, but as the radio voice continued its description he could not move. 'Wearing jeans,' it was saying, 'and a sweater embroidered with a distinctive sunflower design...'

That's her! thought Matty. *That's Greensleeves' Mam*!

His teeth started to chatter and the carton trembled in his cold hands. Flattened against the wall, ears straining, he listened intently to the rest of the news item, repeating it silently to himself, fixing the details in his memory.

Dazed, he watched the water from the tap washing out into the yard, turning to liquid gold where it slid into the light from the farmhouse door. It was not until he heard the man utter a gruff exclamation and the dog begin to bark again that he at last turned to go.

He was half way down the alley way between the buildings when he heard a shout behind him and glancing over his shoulder, saw the silhouette of the farmer, brandishing a stick. Then a shaggy black and white collie came bounding round the corner, splashing through the puddles and yapping wildly.

Clutching his carton, slopping the precious water everywhere, Matty ran.

Chapter 35

To add to his sense that he was not in charge of his own life at the moment, Oliver's car had refused to start. Now, with the afternoon light already waning, he drove along the narrow lanes at reckless speed, relying on his horn and his headlights to warn other vehicles.

It was more than twelve hours since Bella and Matty had turned up at *Guinevere's Bower*. How was he going to explain that gap – even to someone as laid back as Brian Hassell?

Whistling savagely between his teeth he swung round a bend and then stood on his brakes. They squealed like a wounded animal and the car swerved, sashaying across the road before it came to a halt with its nose in the hedge.

Oliver leapt out. In the split second before he braked he had seen a boy, naked scalp like a death's head in the beam of his lights, racing towards him along the lane.

'Matthew!' he shouted. Then, 'Matty!'

There was no answer and for a moment Oliver wondered if he had seen a phantom summoned up by his own anxieties. Across the lane from the car there was a gate into a field and out of the corner of his eye he saw something flutter under the hedge on the far side. His actor's work-outs standing him in good stead he vaulted over the gate and called again.

Matty, who had already been chased every which way by the dog and the farmer, had no breath left. By the time he had given his pursuers the slip he had found himself almost in Stretton and was now making his way back towards the barn and Bella. Every drop of water had long ago spilled out of the carton so he had nothing to offer her. And the news he had overhead was repeating itself over and over in his head like a tune he could not get rid of.

When he realised that the man calling to him out of the dark was Oliver he crept out from under the hedge and waited. Destiny, he decided, was taking over again and the only thing to do was to go along with it.

'You look as though you've been in a rugby scrum,' said Oliver, wrinkling his fastidious nose at the children as they stood shivering beside the fire he had lit in his sitting room. 'Take off those filthy togs and I'll put them in the washing machine!'

He found a tee shirt of his own for Bella to wear and

for Matty a black sweater knitted by his mother. Then he packed Bella off to bed with a hot water bottle and cooked bacon and eggs for himself and Matty.

Balancing his supper on his knees, Matty watched the flames licking up the blackness of the chimney and wondered whether he should tell Bella what he had heard on the farmer's radio. If the news item had been about Mo then she ought to know. But if it had not he would be raising false hopes for her. Besides – and with this realisation Matty's throat tightened so that he could not swallow – there had been nothing in the report to say *how Mo was*…

'You know,' said Oliver, as if he had plugged into Matty's thoughts, 'there's no way I can help you find Bella's mother. It needs all the skills of a sleuth – which I don't have…'

He had played the part of a detective once. A silent, grim, spectral sort of fellow. The kind who lurked in doorways with his collar turned up and his hat brim turned down. Nowadays a detective would probably spend most of his time in a neon lit office with banks of computers. Easy access to the information he needed…

'To begin with,' he went on as Matty did not speak, 'I'd need to know more about Mo, what *kind* of person she is…'

'She's awright,' said Matty. 'Got lots of go in her.'

'So it seems,' said Oliver, drily. He wondered whether, as a single mother under pressure, Mo had simply reached the end of her tether. It happened, he knew. 'Perhaps she just took off on holiday somewhere,' he suggested.

'Na!' exclaimed Matty. 'She didn't have no money. Anyways she were very close with Bella, see. If she'd been goin' to do that she'd of said.'

Uneasy with the knowledge he had not shared with Oliver and uncertain whether he could trust him with it, he jumped up and began to wander about the room.

'Can't you keep still, Matthew?' asked Oliver, whose head was thumping.

When he first recaptured Matty he thought he would take both children straight to Stretton police station. Then he had seen Bella. With her so poorly the only option seemed to be to bring them home. The situation was slipping further and further out of his grasp and what he needed now was quietness, time to think.

'I don't suppose you play chess, do you?' he asked without much hope.

'Yep, I do,' said Matty bouncing back to his seat. 'Dave, one of me foster dads, taught me. He were ace at chess. And at cards…'

Catching the faint echo of regret in Matty's voice Oliver said, 'Right. OK then. Let's see how well he taught you. Lay out the pieces, will you, while I clear up.'

When he returned from the kitchen, Matty was ready and waiting for him.

'You're an actor, ent you?' he asked as Oliver sat down.

'After a fashion. Sometimes.'

'I'm goin' on the stage, when I grows up. Not as an actor though. I'll be an acrobat. Or a juggler. Or mebbe a magician.'

Oliver sighed. Clearly playing chess was not going to stop Matty from talking. 'It's a crazy profession,' he said, sourly. 'I'd think of something else if I were you.'

'Mm. P'raps I'll be a map maker then. I likes maps. Them and PE are what I'm good at, see.'

'Cartwheels and cartography, eh,' said Oliver smiling for the first time and moving a pawn.

Matty scowled. He suspected Oliver was making fun of him and for a while he played in silence. *I got to get away*, he thought. *So long as I'm sure Greensleeves is safe...*

'D'you think it'll snow tonight?' he asked, out of these thoughts. ''Cos if it does we could be stuck here!'

'Heaven forbid!' exclaimed Oliver. And then felt bad because Matty first looked pained and then took his bishop.

SUNDAY

Chapter 36

Bella did not wake until the darkness was growing grainy with the beginning of daylight. Confused by the unfamiliar shapes of the room and the furniture she lay for a long time puzzling over it before she remembered she was back in *Guinevere's Bower*. Oliver's house.

Still only half awake she wondered what Oliver was playing at. Why had he not set the police on their trail? And why, when he accidentally found them again yesterday, had he brought them back to *Guinevere's Bower*? On Friday she had thought him cold, hard, aloof. Yet only twenty-four hours later here he was, looking after them in the caring way she hoped her real father might…

Her head ached with these unanswered questions and she was very thirsty again. On the table beside her bed there was an empty glass and picking it up she crept downstairs to fetch a drink. The kitchen was cold so she moved into the sitting room where the embers of last night's fire still glowed. Kneeling on the carpet she stirred the cinders with a stick until they blazed up.

In the wavering yellow light she looked around the room. It was quite different from the living room at Number 21. Plain white walls. A few softly tinted pictures. Four deep armchairs with pale linen covers and no cushions. And on the darkly polished sideboard one silver framed photograph of an elderly lady with an amused expression and softly curled grey hair.

'Not your sort of room, Mo,' she murmured. 'Too tidy. And too colourless!'

Turning back to face the hearth, she noticed Matty's rucksack under the table where the unfinished chess game was set out. He must have been either very relaxed or very preoccupied to leave it there. Usually he would not let his precious snow globe out of his sight.

Curiously she peeped inside the bag and saw the globe nestling amongst the smelly remains of party food. Drawing it out she polished the smeared glass with the hem of Oliver's tee-shirt. Then, filled with a sudden yearning to have it work some magic for her, she sat down and stared into it. But nothing happened. In the grey dawn light the girl and the tree looked dowdy, faded, faraway.

Disappointed, Bella ran her hands over the cold glass until one of her fingers snagged on the roughness of a flaw. Setting her eye to it she was surprised to find that this time she was looking deep into the heart of the tree. As if it were a living tree she could see the rugged grooves in its bark, the patches of green lichen on its trunk and the intricate knotting of branches where the shaken snow was collecting in tiny drifts. And something else. Something she had never spotted before.

Wedged into the fork of the tree was another child. A boy. Partly masked by the mesh of boughs, his dun-coloured jerkin and trousers blended like camouflage into them. A gleam of light lit up his fair hair but he was facing away from Bella – looking down at the girl in the green coat – and in his raised hand was a snowball.

Or was it the snow globe itself that he held? Was the globe like one of those pictures within a picture where the same scene goes on repeating itself to infinity?

Slowly Bella lowered the globe on to her lap.

Did Matty see himself in the boy as he saw her in the girl? Was that why he felt so sure their destinies were linked? He would never explain exactly what he saw in the globe but she guessed that whatever it was, to him it was very real.

It was like when people saw ghosts, or fairies, or aliens from another planet. You could not be sure that such beings actually existed but neither could you be sure they did not. Perhaps Matty had some extra sixth sense that she and most other people lacked.

'Right, Gosling,' murmured Mo's voice in her head. 'He's one of the Beatified!'

This was a word Mo used when she meant someone who had special gifts. And Bella knew that Matty *was* special. The wretched life he had led should have turned him bad or bitter. But it had not. Instead it seemed to have taught him to understand unhappiness without being darkened by it himself. And although no-one, apart perhaps from his Gran, had ever loved him his own heart stayed warm, loving, caring…

Packing the snow globe carefully back into his bag, Bella stood up. The last of the fire had burned out and she was very cold. As she paused by the window on her way to the stairs, she glanced outside. A fine, fresh powdering of snow had fallen during the night and birds, pecking at crumbs which Oliver had put out, had left black twiggy trails across it.

I wish I were a bird, thought Bella. *Then I could fly far and wide to search for Mo.*

The longing for Mo and home overwhelmed her again and she crawled back to bed where she lay shivering and sweating by turns, until Matty thumped on the door.

Chapter 37

'Strewth!' grumbled Oliver as he slotted bread into his toaster. 'I do believe the girl's still got a temperature. How'm I going to explain things if I have to call a doctor?'

Leaving the kitchen he started to hunt for a thermometer. The only one he could find was the one in his barometer and that, he observed, was set at 'stormy'. Already he could hear Matty awake and jigging about in his study and the prospect of the day ahead appalled him.

'Why,' he asked himself, 'am I *doing* this? Letting myself get involved like this... snared in someone else's story...'

But before he could properly frame the question he knew the answer. It was for the sake of the child he once was, the child who had felt that nobody cared...

Out in the kitchen the smoke alarm shrilled as the bread in the toaster began to burn and as he rushed to quieten it, he bumped into the sideboard and the photograph of his mother wobbled and fell over.

'OK! OK!' he said to her as he set it straight. 'You were right. I was a fool not to call in the proper authorities at the very beginning.'

Flapping a tea towel at the smoke he considered what he might do. Five minutes later he picked up the telephone and dialled a Waterham number.

Leaving her breakfast uneaten, Bella slept once more, a feverish, dream-ridden sleep. When she woke her mother's absence was nagging in her head like an aching tooth.

WHERE ARE YOU, MO? WHERE ARE YOU?

Through red-rimmed eyes she squinted at her watch

and saw it was two o'clock. Sunday was more than half over and Mo had been missing for nearly a week.

Like a cold flame panic seared through her again. She sprang out of bed and wrapping the white duvet around her stumbled downstairs. There was no-one in the kitchen but in the sitting room Matty was lying on his front by the empty hearth. He was wearing Oliver's black sweater pulled over her clean dungarees and he was gazing into his snow globe.

'You're not trying to read your *destiny* again, are you?' she snapped at him. 'Where's Oliver?'

'Gone to Waterham,' said Matty without looking up.

'Why?'

'Dunno. He ent said.'

All morning Oliver had been silent and pre-occupied and Matty, still nursing his secret knowledge, had felt unable to break into that silence. Unbearably restless he had gone into the garden where he built a family of snowmen. Then, at lunchtime, Oliver had announced he was going out for an hour.

As soon as he left Matty played around with the radio in the kitchen, finding the local station and listening until the first news broadcast. But there was no repeat of the item he had overhead in the farmyard.

Now, brooding gloomily over his snow globe, he was shocked out of his reverie when Bella stamped her foot.

'I'll bet he's gone to fetch someone to take us off his hands!' she shouted. 'You and your stupid signs! We're getting into a worse and worse mess. We're no nearer to finding Mo… and my head feels as if it's about to burst!'

Convinced by Bella's distress that he ought to tell her what he thought he had discovered about her mother, Matty stood up. She glared at him and then flounced

143

away to stand staring out of the widow.

Outside the sky seemed to be pressing so close to the earth that it was driving out all the light. From the lawn four snowmen looked back at her with stony eyes and frozen smiles. Fresh snow freckled the scarf tied round the neck of the tallest snowman and glistened on Mo's black wig where it dangled over the eyes of the smallest.

'This place,' cried Bella turning away from them, 'is full of *mimic* men!'

She did not know what she meant by that. The phrase came into her head from nowhere. But it had something to do with her disappointment over Oliver, her feeling that both he and Matty had let her down.

Matty did not know what she meant either but he felt the force of her anger with him. Keeping his head bowed over the globe which he still clutched in his hands, he searched desperately for the right words to begin telling her what he knew. Bella, who wanted a battle, mistook his silence for a sulky refusal to fight back and was goaded to further fury.

'Listen to me,' she raged. 'Listen you horrid, bald, useless boy!'

With a swift, hurt sideways glance he took in the smoulder of her hair, the sparks flashing in her eyes and setting his snow globe down on the table among the chessmen, he took a step towards her.

'Keep away from me!' she shrieked. 'Changeling! Goblin! With your spooky crystal ball and your mad ideas about destiny! You've bewitched me! I'm sick. I'm miles away from home. I'm with two weirdos… oddballs… crazies that I don't know and don't want to know! And I've lost Mo… perhaps for ever…!'

Through the pounding in her head, the fever in her

144

blood, Bella heard the shrill whine of her own voice and was disgusted. Yet she could not stop. All the doubts and fears and angers of the last seven days came tumbling out. And the more she ranted the more furious and miserable she became.

Stung by the unfairness of her attack and still uncertain what to do Matty neither moved nor spoke until Bella, flinging off her duvet, suddenly dodged past him and pounced on his snow globe.

'No!' he cried. 'That ent to blame!'

But snatching it out of his reach Bella pranced across the room, whirling the glass ball around her head until the snowflakes were shaken into a blizzard, filling it like fog.

'See!' she taunted him. 'It isn't magic. It's just a silly, babyish toy!'

'Please,' said Matty, keeping very still. 'Give it back.'

'I bet you stole it!'

'No. It's mine. I told you.'

'Mine,' she mocked. 'Mine. Mine. Mine!'

Panting they faced each other across Oliver's quiet sitting room. Then Bella backed against the window, holding the globe up to the dusky light.

'If you want it,' she said, 'come and get it.'

As she first offered it to him and then withdrew it the glass ball winked and gleamed in the wintry twilight. This play of light on its surface obscured the scene inside it and all Matty could see was the reflection of the world outside, cold and grey and upside down.

Turning away he shook his head and in a new surge of exasperation Bella snarled, 'Catch it then!,' and hurled the globe towards him.

Startled, Matty swung round, reached out for it but his

usually quick reactions were slowed by the heaviness around his heart and he missed. The snow globe struck him full in the chest. Gasping with pain he staggered and went down on one knee. The glass ball rolled across his leg and dropped unharmed on to the deep pile of the carpet.

For a moment neither of them moved. All Bella could hear was the steady tick of Oliver's clock and the roar of her own blood in her ears. Bewildered by the speed with which everything had happened, Matty crouched over the anguish in his chest. He wanted to cry but who was there to comfort him? Shakily, as the pain ebbed, he rose to his feet. Then without a word or a glance to Bella, he scooped up the globe and crept out into the kitchen.

Already stricken with remorse at her own cruelty, Bella yearned to follow him. But something hard and unyielding in her would not let her. It was like when she quarrelled with Mo. She always *felt* sorry but found it impossible to say the words. So instead of going after him she flung herself into the armchair where Matty had been sitting and sat scowling into space.

As if from very far away she heard the back door open and quietly close again. A bitter draught swept around her bare feet. Two minutes later when she went to look, she found that Matty had gone.

Chapter 38

Oliver turned the heating in his car up to full and drummed his fingers on the steering wheel. Snow hurtled towards him, clotting on the windscreen, heaping itself along the wipers until they slowed almost to a stop.

Beyond them he could see nothing except a curtain of white flakes flapping in the wind.

When he reached the village of Bradstock, less than half way to Waterham, he pulled up beside the post office and went into the telephone kiosk outside. Clumsy with the cold he pushed fifty pence into the slot.

'Sorry, Ma,' he said. 'I'm never going to make it.'

Once more he felt that his plans were being thwarted, that he was being forcibly steered away from the direction he wanted to take.

'Damn it,' he said. 'The weather's really dumped me in the mire! I needed you, Ma… needed your nursing skills…'

'Quite apart from that, Son,' his mother said, 'you should have someone else there with you. What you're doing isn't… isn't wise. And if the girl is sick…'

She went on reprovingly while Oliver slouched against the wall of the booth and watched the digits on the machine tick steadily away.

'Ma, darling,' he said. "I haven't enough change to listen to a lecture.'

She stopped and then laughed. 'By the way,' she said. 'Something I was going to tell you. You remember Daventry? The other Oliver we think the girl muddled up with you? Well, I discovered – through my grapevine, you know – that he only lives twelve miles away. He's newly married and working as a car salesman. In Bristowe!'

'Really?' Oliver yawned and straightened up. 'So he never did make the silver screen!'

'Miaow!' said his mother.

The last of his fifty pence flashed up on the dial and telling her he'd ring later from home, Oliver said goodbye.

147

Backing out of the telephone box, his feet slithered on the snow that was already thickening on the pavement.

'That's if,' he muttered, 'I ever get home!'

By the time Oliver turned into the driveway of *Guinevere's Bower* he had been away twice a long as he intended. The blizzard had stopped but the blustery wind was raising little wraiths of snow from the drifts under the hedgerows and every time he touched his foot to the brake he felt the car slide and shimmy.

When at last he slewed to a stop beneath the cedar tree, he was horrified to see Bella standing on the front doorstep. She was wearing her green coat draped like a cape over his thin tee shirt and she looked distraught.

'Matty's disappeared,' she wailed. 'He's run away again!'

Oliver climbed out of the car and the wind whisked coldly between them.

'It's all my fault,' she sobbed. 'I lost my temper and hurt him. Just like I did with Mo. And now he's gone too. And I've got *spots*!'

Oliver hurried her back into the house. It was some time before she calmed down and he was able to establish that the spots had nothing to do with her guilt. Switching on a lamp he examined the inside of her arms where small, bright pink blisters marred the white skin.

'I've no idea what they are,' he said.

Bella scowled, first at him and then at the spots.

'I have,' she said. 'They're chicken pox. I've caught the boggling, snarligogging chicken pox from Ali!'

'I don't know about chicken pox,' exclaimed Oliver, 'but one thing you certainly do have is a picturesque line in swearing!'

★ ★ ★ ★ ★

148

Halfway down the aisle of St Christopher's church, in Owlcombe, Matty sat huddled in the corner of a pew. Apart from the rustle of his own shivering and the hollow winnowing of the wind around the tower, it was very quiet. A last ray of daylight glancing through the window behind the altar, made the face of a stained glass angel glow with life and colour.

Beside him on the seat lay his snow globe, its magic extinguished in the gloom of the church. Like the life in the angel's face that magic was an illusion. A mere trick of the light. Something he had invented to comfort himself and make believe that his life had meaning and purpose.

Matty did not so much think these thoughts as feel them. They throbbed in his chest where the bruise caused by Bella still ached with a tender ache.

The clanking of the heavy latch on the church door broke into the silence. It must be the priest again. Already he had been in once, pacing up the length of the aisle to kneel before the altar. Matty had clenched himself around his shivers and the priest had gone away without noticing him.

This time, expecting a light to flick on, Matty cowered below the back of the seat. But nothing happened. He could hear the soft sound of someone breathing and the scuffle of feet on tiles. Then an arc of light from a torch wavered over the floor before flashing upwards and stroking along the rows of pews. He wriggled further down into the black gap between the seats. His elbow caught the snow globe and it skidded noisily on its stone base, along the wooden bench.

Seconds later, as he scrabbled after it, a strong hand reached down into the darkness and plucked him from his hiding place.

Chapter 39

'You can't *keep* running away like this,' said Oliver. 'In the end you'll simply run into a dead end!'

Drooping under the weight of Oliver's coat Matty said nothing. People who were quite safe where they were, he thought, were always warning him about the dangers of running away. Besides that's not what he was doing. He had left Bella partly to punish her and partly to recover from hurt. But also to *think* – because his knowledge about Mo seemed to be burning a hole in his brain.

Oliver, who had spent an hour trudging round the village, struggled to be patient. He sat jiggling the torch so that its beam trembled over the walls of the nave. From the top of one pillar, a gargoyle with beetling brows and thick lips hanging slack, seemed to glower down at him. It reminded him of his old headmaster.

'I do know about running away,' he said. 'I used to do it regularly when I was your age.'

'Why?' asked Matty, surprised. 'You wasn't poor. And you had a Mam…'

'That's true. But my Dad was in the army, posted abroad, and Ma went with him. So I was sent to boarding school.'

'I bet that weren't as bad as a *Home*, though.'

'Hmm,' Oliver tweaked at his ear lobe. 'Perhaps… perhaps not. But I hated it. I felt abandoned and lonely and horribly homesick. What's more being something of a… of a loner… I was bullied.'

Matty considered this. He could hardly believe that Oliver's experiences were anything like his own.

'Where'd'you run to?' he asked.

'Different places. I never thought much about where I

was going. Just pushed off.'

Oliver's voice went on whispering among the shadows and Matty's thoughts skidded away. Was that, after all, what Bella's Mam had done? Just pushed off and then…?

Raising his head he was about to say something but Oliver, thinking he was showing interest in his story, went on talking.

'My school was in the Midlands,' he said. 'And quite close by – though strictly out of bounds – was the Shropshire Union Canal. To me that canal was as exciting as the sea! Narrow boats and barges constantly coming and going from far away places. Whenever I got the chance I used to sneak down to the marina where they moored up. One day – when I was feeling especially desperate – I was mooching about among the boat people who came ashore to fetch stores or have a drink in the pub, when I heard someone say that a boat called the *Pride of Bridgnorth* was setting off early next morning for Chester.'

'I been to Chester,' said Matty, recalling one of his own escapes and becoming interested.

'Right. Well. I had an aunt in Chester. An aunt I was especially fond of. So for once I knew where I was going to run! I was down at the marina before dawn. I found the boat, crept aboard, and hid under a tarpaulin. It was so easy! The only trouble was, nothing happened. All morning I heard boats arriving and departing but my boat didn't budge. No-one came near her and in the end, cold and hungry and dying for a pee, I had to abandon ship!'

Matty grinned. 'I been caught like that,' he said, 'when I were younger.'

'I found then that it was my own stupid fault,' Oliver

went on. 'Because the boat I stowed away in wasn't the *Pride of Bridgnorth* at all. The name on the bows when I scrambled out and saw it properly in daylight, was the *Bride of the North*!'

Under the warm coat, Matty hugged his snow globe to him.

'You read the signs wrong, see,' he said.

'Precisely,' agreed Oliver.

'I ent sure I got them right, either,' said Matty.

Drawing the globe out he held it in the beam of Oliver's torch. The golden light filled it, touching the snow with warmth, turning the girl's hair to a fiery halo. And with a muffled exclamation, Oliver took it from him.

'What a weird coincidence,' he said, turning it in his hands.

Matty assumed he meant the likeness of the girl in the green coat to Bella and nodded.

'Me Gran says that them – coincidences – are allus signs...'

Haltingly, he explained about signs and the meanings he made from them but Oliver, who felt he was entering deep water without being much of a swimmer, shook his head. He felt dejected. Matty's faith and the courage of both children impressed him. But where could it lead? They were both in impossible situations.

'I think,' he said gently. 'You must be prepared for the worst.'

'I allus is,' said Matty.

Abruptly his thoughts switched back to Mo. He might be ready to face the worst but how could he prepare Bella for it?

The quietness of the church was now being disturbed

by clear sounds of activity from the vestry. Glancing at his watch Oliver saw that the evening service was due to start in ten minutes.

'D'you think you're ready to go back?' he asked.

Matty stood up and Oliver handed him the snow globe.

'Don't drop it,' he said. 'Because although I can't gauge its magical value, I can tell you it's worth a lot of money.'

Intrigued, Matty encircled the globe with his hands. George and Arnie had believed that too, he reflected. Considering it came from his Gran who had never had 'more than two cherry stones to pay the rent with,' he doubted it and said so.

'We'll talk about that later,' said Oliver. 'If we don't leave now we'll be trapped here for another hour and by then, heaven knows what sort of a state Bella will be in.'

'I reckons she often gets into states,' whispered Matty tiptoeing after him down the aisle.

'Yes,' agreed Oliver. 'I reckon perhaps she does!'

Chapter 40

When Oliver went to prepare the supper, Bella fussed over Matty, drawing an armchair close to the re-lit fire in the sitting room and insisting he sit there.

I will never, ever hurt him like that, again, she thought. *How could I, who hate cruelty, have been so cruel?*

She winced at the memory and because her shame made her shy with him she did not ask him where he had been but chattered about the book she had been reading while she waited for Oliver to bring him back. It was an illustrated copy of *Wuthering Heights* and the only book she

153

could find on Oliver's shelves that she fancied reading.

'It's cool,' she said. 'It's about a traveller who can't get home because of bad weather and has to stay in this spooky house with a crowd of crazy people…'

The echo of her own earlier words to Matty made her blush and stammer to a stop. Matty, who seemed not to have noticed, silently turned the pages, then paused to study the picture of a barren hilltop where a girl in a long green dress clung to a windswept tree…

Escaping to the kitchen Bella asked Oliver if she could help with the cooking.

'Nothing to do,' he said. 'We're having frozen pizzas.'

'I thought you were a great cook,' she said slily, thinking of the Golden Sunbursts commercial.

'Only in the Land of Pretend,' said Oliver.

We're all in the Land of Pretend now, thought Bella. She wondered whether, if Oliver had been her father, he would have seemed more *real* to her. Even Mo, her faults and virtues so familiar, was suddenly a mystery, a stranger. Her disappearance had altered everything Bella felt she knew about her. Perhaps it was impossible ever to truly know another person…

The furious itching of her spots brought Bella back to earth. She knew she shouldn't scratch them so she slapped them as though she were swatting flies.

'Strewth,' said Oliver, banging the pizzas into the oven, 'will you stop that!'

Then he went to ring his mother as he had promised.

'If you've no calamine lotion,' she said, 'try ice cubes.'

So Bella sat at the table with a saucer of ice cubes which she dabbed on the spots she could reach. It did not help the itching much but it made Matty laugh and set them talking again.

154

The wind was making a ceaseless chatter in the old window casements and after supper, while Oliver sprawled exhausted in his chair and Matty lay on the carpet, she read them the chapter of *Wuthering Heights* where Cathy's ghost taps on the window and cries piteously to be let in. Enjoying the sound of her voice and the dramatic way she read, Matty tried to listen. But long before she had finished both he and Oliver were asleep.

The story which soothed them, however, disturbed Bella. Whenever she tried to picture Cathy she saw Mo, her face wan, desperate, streaked with tears.

Blowing on her burning arms, she dropped the book. The wind rattled Oliver's letter box and howled about the walls of Guinevere's Bower like a soul in pain. She went to the window and twitched aside the curtain. Snow was spinning towards her out of the dark, flakes flying every which way like scraps of torn paper tossed into the gale. Already it was piling up against the window panes and out on the lawn it swathed the heads of Matty's snowmen in cold white bandages.

She jumped as Oliver appeared beside her.

'What are you going to do with us?' she asked.

'Take you back to Orbury,' said Oliver, judging for the second time that it was best to be brutally honest with her. 'I have no choice. For the sake of your mother we can't mess about any longer.'

Concerned above all now about Mo, Bella did not protest.

'But what about Matty,' she murmured, 'having to go back to the Home? They'll punish him, I know they will because...'

'No,' said Oliver. He leaned closer to the window and his breath spread fingers of cloud on the glass. 'I shall deliver him to Elmbridge House myself,' he continued firmly. 'That way I can make sure they know… and make sure *he* knows too… that from now on I shall be keeping an eye on him.'

Puzzled but pleased, Bella turned and smiled at him. The smile, Oliver thought, transformed her face, making it beautiful.

'It'll have to be tomorrow,' he said, gently. 'Tuesday I'm supposed to be in college.'

Retreating to the hearth, he threw another log on the fire. The wood crackled and flared, the flames sucked high up the chimney by the wind and it occurred to him that unless the weather changed, his plans once more would be thwarted. The same thought struck Bella and she remembered with a queasy sensation how in her temper she had stirred up a tempest in Matty's snow globe.

'I'm sorry, Matt,' she said.

Her voice, loud in the quietness, woke him. He rolled over, stretched and sat up.

'What?' he said. 'Ent there anythin' for supper?'

MONDAY

Chapter 41

At half-past seven on Monday morning Oliver opened the back door and the drifted snow, like a heap of cold white feathers, slid into the room and buried his feet. Cursing he shovelled it out with the dustpan and forced the door shut. His trouser bottoms were sopping and he was just about to go and change them when Matty, fully dressed, dashed into the kitchen.

'The road's blocked,' he said. 'And I *has* to get out.'

'You're not planning on running away again!' exclaimed Oliver.

'It ent that.'

Matty blinked and fidgeted, shuffling from one foot to the other. Exasperated but sensing there was something else he wanted to say, Oliver abandoned the idea of going to change, pulled a stool from under the table and sat down.

'What is it?' he said.

Independent as he was, Matty recognised when he could not deal with things on his own. He had intended making his way to Bristowe and following up the clues he had gleaned from the radio but he could see there was no help for it now. He would have to tell Oliver what he knew. Uncertain that he would be believed, however, he still hesitated.

'Tell you what,' said Oliver. 'Let's start clearing the path to the gate. We shall be that much nearer getting out and you can talk to me while we work.'

Overnight the landscape had been transformed, its humps levelled, its hollows filled, with radiant white. But the snow had stopped and over Owlcombe Brake, the sky was streaked with pink and silver light where the sun was trying to break through.

'It's got to be her, see,' said Matty, stopping to clear his spade. 'All that about short red hair and blue eyes...'

'And you say she was in *Bristowe*?' said Oliver.

'Yep. In the Royal... the Royal...'

'Royal Victoria Hospital. And unconscious?'

'For a whole week. That's just the time she's been missin', ent it?'

'You still can't assume it's her. Quite a lot of people have red hair and...'

'Yeah – but what about the sunflower on her jumper! Greensleeves' Mam has sunflowers everywhere. She thinks they're really cool. Somethin' to do with a bloke called Van Goff...'

Oliver straightened up and felt the freezing air scour his hot face.

'All the same,' he said. 'Why would Bella's Mum be in *Bristowe*?'

Even as he spoke he remembered what his mother had said about Oliver Daventry and thought it odd that Mo's name should twice in two days be mentioned in connection with Bristowe.

'Are you sure you haven't imagined this, Matthew?' he asked. '*I* haven't heard anything...'

'I knowed you'd say that,' grunted Matty hurling a spadeful of snow into the middle of Oliver's favourite shrub. 'But I ent imagined anythin'. I *heard* it. And I reckons you don't listen to the radio much. Not Radio Bristowe, anyways...'

By lunchtime Oliver and Matty had cleared a path down the drive to the gate. Throughout the whole morning no traffic passed Guinevere's Bower. It was as still and silent as the beginning of the world.

While Matty scrambled eggs with cheese, and grilled tomatoes, Oliver listened to the local news. But all he learned was that most of the main roads into Bristowe had been cleared of snow.

'I think you should go back to bed this afternoon,' he said to Bella as they finished eating.

'Why?' she protested. 'I feel fine.'

Oliver insisted. Bella was about to retort that as he was not her father he could not tell her what to do when she caught Matty's eye.

'Oh, all right,' she sighed. And collecting *Wuthering Heights* from the sitting room she went.

Matty bounced up and down, making his chair jump and jiggle on the tiled floor. 'A troubled shared, Matty,' he could hear his Gran say, 'is a trouble halved.' And indeed, having told Oliver his secret, he felt as if a great burden had been lifted off his shoulders.

'When can we set off?' he demanded.

Oliver frowned and tugged his ear. Matty's off-loaded burden filled *him* with doubt and dread. He had rung the hospital in Bristowe but over the telephone they would tell him nothing more than he already knew.

'D'you think she's bad with chicken pox?' asked Matty to whom this thought had just occurred.

'For heaven's sake!' exclaimed Oliver. 'You don't go into a coma with chicken pox! It must be something much more serious.'

'That's what I reckons,' said Matty. 'That's why I didn't tell Bella, see.'

For a moment Oliver did not respond. Then he said, 'You were right not to. And I'm not at all sure I should be taking you with me either.' He saw himself standing in a white walled mortuary, Matty at his side, and shuddered.

Matty who had already considered this possibility, noticed and guessed what Oliver was thinking.

'It's awright,' he said. 'Anyways, I got to come. I'm the only one as knows her, ent I?'

Oliver looked at him, thoughtfully. With his hair beginning to grow and his clothes clean Matty looked more like a normal ten-year-old. But he was stronger than most ten-year-olds. If what they discovered turned out to be bad he would probably cope.

Standing up, Oliver crossed to the window and stared out at the lifeless white wilderness.

'Right,' he said. 'Nevertheless, I shouldn't be too hopeful about anything. To begin with, there isn't a chance of leaving here until – or unless – the snowplough arrives.'

Chapter 42

'I must have been mad!' said Oliver. 'The roads are deadly. And this is surely a fool's errand…'

He crouched over the steering-wheel and the car crawled out of Owlcombe. On either side the snow was heaped hedge high so that it was like driving through a roofless white tunnel.

Hunched beside him Matty rolled his snow globe between his hands, feeling the faint warmth radiating from it.

'D'you take that snow globe with you everywhere?' asked Oliver, irritably.

'Yep. It's precious.'

'Far too precious to cart about like that!'

Matty thought about this. For him the snow globe was precious because it was a gift from his Gran, a link with the good times of his own past. But also it held a promise for the future. Its images, the girl, the boy, the tree, the robin, were frozen into a single moment of their story. Under a spell of snow. Yet in the globe's magically changing light and mood they seemed to stir and breathe. So that you knew, when the story moved on, *they* would move on. The sun would shine, the snow would thaw, the tree would put out leaves. And for the children too a new life would begin. Nothing had to stay the same for ever...

The car slithered as Oliver changed gear and he swore under his breath.

'You said you'd tell me somethin' you knowed about me snow ball,' said Matty. 'When we was in the church you said it.'

Oliver stared straight ahead, his eyes baffled by the glare of his headlights on the snow. He did not feel like talking.

'Go on,' pleaded Matty.

'I've seen one before. That's all.'

Matty was cast down. He thought his snow globe was the only one like it in the world.

'Well,' Oliver said, 'the one I saw wasn't *identical*. The tree was different and there was no girl. Only an old shepherd with his dog. But the figures were beautifully detailed and the snow, like yours, was starry white crystals. Not a bit like the crumbly bits of polystyrene you get in modern snowglobes.'

'Where d'you see it?'

'In an antique shop in Paris. This was years ago, mind. It was locked away in a cabinet and I asked to have a closer look at it. The antique dealer told me it was made early in the last century by a Swiss artist who lived in the High Alps. He did tell me his name. Jaques something or other…'

'Yeah! Cool!' exclaimed Matty, bouncing again and running his fingers over the flat base of the rock in which the glass was set. 'It must be the same bloke! I see the J – and a S and a Y – scratched into the stone…'

'Right,' said Oliver, pleased. 'That was it! His name was Jaques St Yves. He didn't make many globes – and they weren't meant as toys.'

'No,' said Matty. 'And I reckons he weren't just an artist either. He were a *magician*.'

They had reached the junction with Stretton's main street and Oliver saw with relief that here the cleared road had been gritted.

'Yes… well… There was magic in his skill,' he said. 'And in his imagination too. I'll give you that.'

Shrugging the stiffness out of his shoulders, he leaned back and accelerated. Grit spurted from under his wheels and the car shot forward under the lights.

'Why didn't you buy that one in Paris?' asked Matty. 'Been as you liked it so much?'

There was a long pause before Oliver said, 'I liked it all right. The problem was, I couldn't *begin* to afford it!'

Sitting by the dead ashes of the fire, Bella felt like Cinderella, deserted by people with more exciting things to do.

'Where are you going?' she had demanded of Oliver.

'Bristowe.'

'Why can't I come?'

'You know why. You're not well enough.'

'I don't see why Matty should go. Leave Matty with me.'

'I need him. He might have to help dig me out of a snow drift.'

'What are you going *for* – on a night like this? What if it snows again and you can't get back?'

'On an important errand for a friend. And it won't,' said Oliver, answering both questions as briefly as possible.

Now Bella tried to read. But this evening *Wuthering Heights* seemed too sad and its haunting mood unsettled her. Used to being on her own at night she was not precisely scared but *Guinevere's Bower*, wrapped in snow and silence, felt very lonely. She missed the noise of the traffic on Upper Park Road and the comforting sound of Mrs Parker moving about next door. Here the husky tick of the grandfather clock, the creaks and groans of the house's old timbers all began to make her feel jumpy.

She switched on the television. Coronation Street was just finishing and she was about to try another channel when the first commercial started. It was the one for Golden Sunbursts.

Watching it, Bella realised she would never be able to see it in the same way again. For behind the screen Oliver there would always be the shadow of the real man. Darker and more difficult. Worried, uncertain, plagued by his conscience. And somehow shut away inside himself. He had a wry sense of humour but was not funny as she had expected him to be. With her, especially, he was awkward and reserved. Though much more at ease with Matty.

Not Mo's kind of man, she thought.

Then, although there was nothing she wanted to watch, she left the television on. To keep the ghosts at bay. And to stop herself from thinking. Because all thinking now led back to Mo and swept Bella away on a wave of fear and misery.

Chapter 43

The Royal Victoria Hospital was a towering, grey building in the centre of Bristowe. There were no spaces in the car park and Oliver had to leave the car several streets away. Here in the city the snow had already disappeared leaving only blackened heaps along the pavements, heaps which seemed to breathe out a dank, raw air.

By contrast inside the hospital it was warm and stuffy. Looking along the crowded, brightly lit corridors, Oliver dithered. It was Matty who found the reception desk.

'There've been lots of enquiries about this lady,' said the receptionist frowning at them over the top of her spectacles. 'What is *your* interest in her?'

Oliver was trying to shape an answer when Matty said, 'We thinks she might be me Mam. Me Mam's gone missin,' see.'

The receptionist stared hard at him. Under the neon lights his stubble of hair shone golden red.

'What's your mother's name?' she asked.

'Morag Partridge,' said Oliver.

'And you, sir? Are you Mr Partridge?'

Matty snickered and Oliver said hastily he was just a family friend.

The woman took his name and address and then, while Matty hopped from one foot to the other, she riffled through a pile of papers, answered the telephone twice, dealt with another enquiry. At last, after making a 'phone call herself, she leant forward.

'You can go up,' she said. 'It's Ward 18.'

They trekked along corridors, went up four floors in a lift, trailed along more corridors. Oliver's hands were sweating. Matty's faith that the woman they had come to see would be Bella's mother had infected him earlier on but now he was full of doubt.

Matty trotted close beside him. He hated hospitals. The heat, the smell, the hushed busyness, the half-closed doors through which you caught glimpses of strange and scary machinery. Once, when he was very little, his Gran had taken him into a hospital. And there, lying in a neat, white bed, looking like a stranger, was his mother. As soon as she saw them she started to cry. She held Matty's hand in her limp, cool fingers and all she did was to cry and to cry…

When they found Ward 18 there were visitors sitting around most of the beds. Oliver and Matty walked slowly, pausing to study every face. An old lady smiled and waved. A young one with no visitors told them to stop staring and push off. They were almost at the end of the ward and there was no one who looked in the least like Mo. Oliver spoke to a nurse.

'Ah,' she said. 'Yes. The receptionist rang to say you were coming.' And she showed them a cubicle hidden behind white curtains. From somewhere a little breeze shook the curtains, making them billow and clink on their runners.

The nurse held Matty's arm.

'You mustn't be too disappointed if she's not your Mum,' she said. 'We've no idea who she is or where she comes from. No one's recognised her yet.'

'What happened to her?' asked Oliver. 'Is she badly hurt?'

'Apparently she fell down a flight of steps. No bones broken. But she's fractured her skull and she's deeply unconscious.'

Warning them that the patient was connected up to a feeding tube, the nurse raised her hand to push the curtains back. Unable to bear the suspense a moment longer Matty ducked under her arm and dashed through.

The woman in the bed lay propped up on pillows. Her face was very white and her eyes were closed. A plastic tube inserted in her nose led back to a machine on a trolley. Her hands lay absolutely still on the red coverlet and across her forehead was a straight crimson scar, prickly with stitches and shadowed with a bruise. Her fringe had been combed away from the scar and pinned back with two kirby grips.

Matty stared down at her as Oliver and the nurse came forward.

'Well?' asked the nurse, softly.

Before Matty could answer, the woman's eyelids quivered and he saw a flash of blue beneath her lashes. She stirred and moaned, murmuring something like someone talking in their sleep.

'That's the first sound she's made,' said the nurse, moving swiftly to the bedside. 'Did you hear what she said?'

Matty clutched his snow globe closer to his side.

'Yeah,' he whispered, licking his dry lips. 'I reckons what she said were… "Bella"!'

TUESDAY

The thaw began. Slowly at first. The drifts of snow turned lacey at their edges and water, dripping off the branches of the cedar tree beside *Guinevere's Bower*, drilled tiny holes in the snow still lying beneath it. The air was damp, the sky heavy with unshed rain.

Matty, his cheerfulness fully restored, raced about the lawn, pelting his dwindling snow family with snowballs. By the time he came in his clothes were soaked through and he had to wear Oliver's sweater again. When he opened the door to Mrs Montford his head was wrapped in a towel and she thought he was Bella.

'Sorry I had to ask you to come, Ma,' said Oliver, tweaking hard at his ear. 'Only I must go into college today and I don't want to leave them alone. I hope you'll be OK. Matthew's uncontainable this morning and Bella's like the weather – unsettled to stormy!'

'I want to see Mo,' cried Bella. 'That's all!' Now that Mo had been found she felt she simply could not bear another day without her. 'She asked for me,' she went on. 'If I could sit with her and hold her hand I'm sure she'd get better quicker...'

'More quickly,' corrected Oliver, absently. He had been through this a dozen times already. 'If I take you to the hospital with an infectious disease,' he said, 'they'll have my guts for garters!'

'I can't be infectious any longer,' she wailed. "I feel fine and the spots are drying up!'

'Possibly,' said Oliver, picking up his coat and brief case. 'But the scabs make you look like Frankenstein's monster before its joins had healed.'

Bella burst into tears and stamped out of the room.

★ ★ ★ ★ ★

From the moment Mrs Montford took over, the house seemed to change gear. She found out what quiet things Matty liked to do and then sat him at the kitchen table with paper and coloured pencils to draw her a map of Owlcombe. She brushed Bella's hair and dabbed calamine on the last of her itching spots. Quietly and reassuringly she talked about Mo.

'Oliver was out cold for four days, once,' she said. 'He was playing wicket-keeper in a game of cricket. The batsman missed the ball and in a fit of temper flung his bat in the air. It struck Oliver over the left eye. He has the scar to this day. But he recovered you see – none the worse for it!'

Without fuss, she washed Matty's wet clothes, made them both creamy hot chocolate mid-morning, and toasted cheese and ham sandwiches for lunch.

Bella calmed down. After all Mo had been found. She was not lying dead under a hedge somewhere. She had not flown off to Canada – or to some far away tropical island. If her being in Bristowe was a mystery it was a mystery which would quite soon be solved. When Oliver rang the hospital early that morning they told him Mo had spoken again. Slowly but surely she was coming round.

'She's always been a bit accident prone,' Bella said, remembering Mo's frequently cut or crushed fingers, the splinters, the bruises, the grazed knees and twisted ankles.

Mrs Montford smiled, her eyes crinkling up at the corners, her cheeks dimpling. She looked, thought Bella, like a story book grandmother and for one last, fleeting moment she regretted that Oliver was not her father.

Matty finished his map and began another one for Bella. He was a little wary of Oliver's mother. She reminded him of the women magistrates he had encountered. The excitement of finding Mo trickled away and he was troubled about what was to happen next.

They'll take me back, he thought. *To Elmbridge House.*

Nevertheless, he devoured Mrs Montford's toasted sandwiches as though he had never seen food before and even finished off the one that Bella could not manage.

Chapter 45

When Oliver visited Mo that evening, he went alone.

'She's still very dopey,' said the nurse. 'But she's coming back. It's a pity you didn't bring her little boy tonight. That would have done her good.'

Mo lay with her eyes closed but at least the tube had been removed from her nose and there was a faint flush of colour in her cheeks.

'She hasn't got a son,' said Oliver, forgetting Matty's fib of the previous night. 'She has a daughter, Bella, but…'

'Bella,' murmured Mo. Her eyes flickered open and she looked about her as if expecting to see her daughter.

'It's OK,' said Oliver drawing a chair up to the bed. 'Bella's fine.'

The nurse left and Mo stared at him in silence. Her eyes were wide and dark with fatigue. Uncomfortable under such scrutiny, Oliver smiled, coughed, ran his hands through his hair and was about to explain who he was when she said, 'Monty!'

'So you know…' he began.

'Golden Sunbursts' she said. 'And the nurse told me. Mr Oliver Montford she said, coming to see me. But I can't see how… that is *why*… I mean…'

Her voice trailed away and she rolled her head restlessly on the pillow as if angry with herself for not being able to find the words she wanted.

In a fumbling, stumbling way Oliver started to tell her the story of the last few days. Of Bella's and Matty's adventures and of how he had been drawn into them. He knew he was talking too much but once started he did not know where to stop. Mo's eyelids kept drooping so that he was not sure how much she heard or understood. Lying there, only half in this world, she looked as young as her daughter.

'Are you saying,' she interrupted him suddenly, 'that Bell thought you were her *father*?'

'Well,' said Oliver. 'Yes. And no. I'm not sure she altogether believed it!'

'Poor Gosling,' muttered Mo, her fingers twisting in the sheet.

'I think she's quite happy to find I'm not,' said Oliver.

Mo made a soft burbling sound that might have been a laugh or a sob and then lapsed back into sleep. Ten minutes later, just as Oliver decided he should leave, she came round again and in a broken tumble of words, told him how she had come to Bristowe on impulse.

'Actually,' she said, looking embarrassed. 'It was to see Bella's father…'

Oliver's eyebrows kinked right up to his hair line. Thinking that his mother had been right and that Oliver Daventry must be Bella' father, he wondered what he should say. He did not want Mo to think he had been prying into her life. Mo, however, read his silence as disapproval.

'First ever time,' she went on hastily. 'Needed some help. Bell so longed for a bike for her birthday and I hadn't *any* money. Hopeless, you know! Never do…'

'Did… er… did he… did Bella's father help?' stammered Oliver.

He could not imagine how Bella – if she discovered the truth – would react to all this. But Mo shook her head and her lips twitched upwards in a half smile.

'Oh didn't see him,' she said. 'No. Changed my mind. Better let lying dogs sleep, I thought! Instead went straight back to the bus station and then…'

She frowned and struggled to sit up but flopped back with a groan, pressing both hands to her temples. 'Scarecrow head,' she said. 'Stuffed with straw. But *aches* like human sort!'

As if on cue the nurse came back, swishing briskly through the curtains. 'I think you should leave, Mr Montford,' she said. 'Miss Partridge will be getting too tired.'

Once more Mo made a laughing sound and for a moment the shadows lifted from her eyes. 'Tired!' she said. 'You told me I'd slept for a week!'

'You had a nasty bang,' said the nurse. 'You fell down a whole flight of concrete steps. Really cracked your head.'

'Cracked long ago,' Mo sniffled. 'They couldn't knock any sense out of it! Perhaps they knocked some *in*.'

'They?' said the nurse, raising her eyebrows at Oliver.

'The boys,' said Mo. 'The ones who snatched my bag at the bus station and pushed me… heigh-ho, tip over top… *you* know…'

'No,' said the nurse. 'We didn't know. But it's true you had no bag when you were brought in. Which is why we'd no idea who you were.'

'I'm nobody,' giggled Mo. 'Who are you?'

Oliver laughed and the nurse said, 'Coming round affects some people that way – like they're a bit tipsy.'

'I know who he is, though,' said Mo nodding at Oliver. 'He's Mr Toad.'

The nurse looked startled and Oliver explained that long ago he had played the part of Toad in 'Toad of Toad Hall'.

'As soon as I can I'll bring her daughter in to see her,' he whispered.

'Oh wondrous,' said Mo, slurrily. 'Good old Mr Toad!'

WEDNESDAY

Bella laid the bunch of snowdrops from Oliver's garden on Mo's bedside table and placed her finger on her lips to warn Matty that her mother was asleep. With exaggerated quietness he tiptoed towards her and then stopped to stare at Mo.

'If she still had her long hair she'd be like the Sleepin' Beauty,' he whispered.

The curtains around the bed were half drawn back today and they could see down the ward to where Mrs Montford stood talking to the nurse. After a few minutes she waved to them before disappearing to do some shopping.

'She said we could only have a measly half-hour,' sighed Bella.

She wondered if Mo would wake up in that time. She looked so dead asleep. Her face was softened and smoothed by sleep, pale except for the redness of the scar which was now without stitches and beginning to heal.

Matty shuffled closer to Bella and Mo opened her eyes. For a second she looked puzzled. Then with a wide smile she sat up, and stretching her arms wide, hugged them both.

'Wondrous,' she crooned, burying her nose in Bella's hair and sniffing the cold fresh air trapped in it. 'I thought Monty wouldn't let you come,' she said hoarsely, releasing them at last. 'He said on the 'phone this morning you were still too spotty…'

'Yep,' said Matty, plumping down on the bed. 'But when he drove off to Orbury his Mam did a sneaky one, see. She rung the hospital…'

'And they said it would be all right,' concluded Bella.

'So she brought us herself this afternoon.'

'How kind of her!' Mo straightened up and sat blinking a little as though it was hard to keep her eyes open.

Bella offered her a bunch of snowdrops. 'Matty picked them for you,' she said.

Tenderly her mother touched the fragile white bells. 'They're beautiful,' she said. 'Thank you.' Her glance lingered on Matty who looked steadily back at her. His hair was now a thick golden stubble, the scars and bruises on his face and scalp almost – but not quite – invisible. Mo, who felt as passionate about cruelty as Bella did, shivered. 'So Monty has gone to Orbury today?' she said.

'Yes.' Bella too sat on the bed, snuggling into the crook of Mo's arm. 'But he was a real old *snarlygogs* before he left!'

'I reckons he was skeered,' said Matty. ''Cos he was goin' to see that witchy Mrs Jenkins at the shop – and your teacher…'

He snickered and then went suddenly quiet and thoughtful. For Oliver was also going, was *mainly* going, to Elmbridge House.

Seeing his change of mood and guessing the reason, Mo reached across Bella and took his hand, pressing the snowdrops into it. 'I'd hate to see these die, Matty!' she said. 'Will you go and ask the nurse for a vase and some water?'

Glad to have something to do Matty jumped off the bed and charged up the ward.

'Is he very upset, Gosling?' Mo asked Bella. 'I mean having to go back to the Home? I wish…'

'If he is,' said Bella, 'he won't show it. Matty's the bravest person I know.' She was just searching for the words to explain to Mo about Matty, about his certainty that he would not be at Elmbridge House for ever, about his belief in himself and his destiny, when she realised they only had ten minutes left. It was better to leave all that for another time. Till Mo was back home and properly well. 'He trusts Oliver too,' she went on. 'He doesn't trust many grown-ups but he knows Oliver will keep his promise...'

'What promise?'

'That things are going to be different for him at the Home from now on. Because Oliver will see that they are...'

'Do *you* trust Monty, Bell?'

'Yes,' said Bella simply.

Mo slid down the bed, turning her face into the pillow. 'When I'm better, Gosling,' she said, 'I promise to tell you about the other Oliver... about your real father.'

Bella shook her head. One day, when she was old enough to deal with it, she would find out about her father. But for now she was contented to have things as they were. Just as long as she had Mo. And Matty.

'D'you remember the story about the Changeling you used to tell me, Mo?' she asked. 'Well, I think Matty's a sort of Changeling. Only he's not the boy left behind by the goblins. He's the *human* one they stole away. He knows he's somehow in the wrong life and he's determined to find his way back to the right one.'

'You care a lot for that boy, don't you?' Mo murmured.

Recalling how she had once felt superior to Matty, a flush of shame rose to Bella's cheeks. How proud, and pleased with herself, she had been when she rescued him from the Gang! And the same later on when she had let him stay with her at Number 21.

'He... he's taught me so much,' she stammered. 'He has

a... he has an *understanding* imagination. And he never gives up! Last week without Matty I wouldn't... I couldn't...'

Mo's hand crept up and covered hers. 'Dearest Bell,' she said. 'I'm sorry about all this. You must have had a really rotten time. You seem older than when I last saw you. Is it really only ten days? But you seem sadder too. You mustn't be sad!'

The words echoed Bella's own thoughts about Mo and she wondered if from here on they were both going to start growing up – together. 'I'm not sad,' she said. 'Not now! I'm *happy* because I've found you. Besides if I hadn't lost you I might not have found Matty. As well as if it wasn't for Matty I might not have found you...'

'Oh!' groaned Mo, 'that's too complicated for me today. It does my poor head in!'

Bella laid cool fingers across her mother's brow and at the same time saw Matty approaching up the ward. In one hand he carried a glass crammed with snowdrops. With the other he was helping to steer an old lady towards her bed. 'Hey, Greensleeves,' he shouted, making the old lady jump and all heads turn. 'She's back! Oliver's Mam's back. She says we got to go!'

'And when you got to go,' giggled Mo, giving Bella a little push, 'you got to go!'

Matty whizzed round the bed and set the flowers on Mo's table.

'Every time I look at them,' she said, smiling drowsily at him. 'I'll think of you. I'll remember how you rescued Bella. And how you found *me*...'

'I'll come back soon, Mo,' whispered Bella, standing up.

'Me too!' cried Matty, whirling out again through the

curtains.

'Oh yes,' murmured Mo, sinking once more into sleep. 'You too! Bella loves you, so I shall surely... of course... come *both* back soon...'

Chapter 47

Bella sat by the window in Oliver's sitting room, her knees pressed against the warm radiator, her book propped on the window ledge. She wanted to finish *Wuthering Heights* before leaving *Guinevere's Bower*. But after the outing to Bristowe and the excitement of seeing Mo, she was tired and finding it hard to concentrate.

It was late afternoon. From the kitchen she could hear the dull thud of a knife striking wood as Matty helped Mrs Montfort to chop vegetables.

She rubbed her eyes and stared out into the rain-grey light. The wind had swung into the west today and heavy showers lashed the garden. The snow was melting away fast. Small avalanches kept sliding off the roof and thudding onto the drive and out on the lawn she could see Matty's snowmen shrunk to shapeless lumps of ice.

Matty. Oliver said he had thought that was a girl's name and she should call him by his proper one. But Matty was the name she knew him by and it was hard to change it. And she *did* know him. She felt she knew him better than anybody else in the world except Mo. Even better than Ali, though she'd known Ali since she was five...

As though her thoughts had conjured him up, there was a bang on the kitchen door and Matty burst through it.

'Oliver's Mam wants to know if you likes roast

chicken,' he said. 'She's doin' a special supper for when Oliver comes home tonight.'

'Yum,' said Bella, setting aside her book.

He called back to Mrs Montford and then came to lean against Bella's chair. Squinting over her shoulder, he said, 'There ent much left of me snowmen.'

'No,' she agreed. 'They're more like snow mice now!'

Matty gurgled with laughter. He was full of high spirits at the turn things were taking. He had encountered so many people in his life who were supposed to care for him but had failed him that he had learned to be cautious. But he knew he could trust Bella – and he had growing confidence in Mo and Oliver too. By holding fast to his dreams and taking note of the signs, he had brought them together. Now they were his friends, his allies. They would not let him go back alone into the uncaring world.

Through the window he could see the clouds beginning to fray apart and bars of silvery light spread like a fan between earth and sky.

'Greensleeves,' he said.

'Yes?'

'When we leaves here I wants you to take me snow ball.'

Bella shook her head. A strange mixture of feelings churned inside her.

'I can't, Matt,' she protested. 'It's your most precious thing! You need it for… For you it's *magic*!'

Without answering her he left the room and she heard him galloping up the stairs. Minutes later he came back with the globe. It was carefully packed now in bubble wrapping, inside a box which Oliver had given to him. Placing the box on her lap, he said, 'The magic'll allus be

190

there. And it's safer with you, see. Anyways I don't need it so much now. 'Cos I can visit, can't I? Come and see it... see *you*...'

'Often and often,' said Bella. 'Whenever you want to!'

Green eyes met green eyes and they both smiled.

'That's awright then,' he said.

Out in the kitchen they heard the clash of pans and the sound of gushing water.

'Hey! I was s'posed to be doin' that,' shouted Matty, dashing for the door. 'We're makin' soup for starters!'

When he left her the brightening light in the room seemed for a moment to go flat and dull. Lifting the globe from its box Bella peeled away the plastic packing.

His destiny, she thought. *In my keeping*.

She held the globe close to her eyes, yearning to see in it the hopeful visions Matty saw.

Disturbed by the tremble in her hands, the snow rose in a flurry around the tree. Through the spinning flakes she thought she saw the girl turn, the skirts of her green coat flaring out, one booted foot lifting and pointing as if she were preparing to dance. And in the net of branches above her, the red-breasted bird fluffed out its feathers. Far, far away, on the very edge of hearing, Bella was sure she heard it whistle. Three clear, sweet notes.

Half scared, half excited, she revolved the globe and put her eye to the flaw on the other side. Faster and faster the snow spun and through it she watched the boy perched in the fork of the tree lean slowly down and toss his snowball towards the girl...

Bella's eyes blurred — as they do if you stare at something too long and too hard — and instead of the scene inside the crystal ball she saw herself and Mo. They were holding hands and swinging their arms, skipping and dancing along Pavilion Street. Dancing home. While there, hopping about on the step of Number 21, was a boy with flopping red-gold hair and a grin that stretched from ear to ear.

Could it *really* ever be like that, she wondered.

'Not easily, Gosling,' whispered Mo's voice in her ear. 'But with time and patience and determination... conceivably... possibly... maybe... perhaps...'

Smiling, still lost in her dream, Bella jumped when Matty again appeared at her side. Carefully he lifted the snow globe from her hands and held it up to the window. The pale winter sunshine filled it with champagne light where the snowflakes rose and fizzled like bubbles.

'I reckons everythin's goin' to work out, ent it?' he said.

'I reckon it is!' Bella said softly. 'Everything's going to be fine.'